THE CESSATION

CHRISTIAN BRINKMAN

CHRISTIAN BRINKMAN

ISBN-10: 0692057110
ISBN-13: 978-0692057117

DEDICATION

To all those who supported me through these many years of writing my first novel. Family, friends, teachers, and all those in-between.

CONTENTS

ACKNOWLEDGMENTS

A huge thanks to everyone who helped me bring my passion to life. To my editor Chersti Nieveen, who assisted me with the structure of my narrative, and guided my final edits. The cover of this novel was created by the amazing hand of artist Jeff Brown. Last, but not least, is my Aunt Sheri, who did the final proofread of my manuscript. I could never have done this without the support of these individuals, as well as my friends and family.

0
29th June 2701 15:46:05

Over half of the ship lost its oxygen supply, corridors freezing throughout and killing most of the crew. The starship *Caroline* just barely held, under too much pressure and starved of the hands used to maintain her. She was dying, and there was nothing Christopher could do to save her.

He stood on the command deck, the shining silver captains badge on his chest reflecting the starlight. Pain swelled in his chest with each shallow breath of the remaining life support.

The pain worsened as he glared through the viewport, debris and corpses floating serenely through the void of space. He let out a deep sigh, turning to face the data table in the center of the spacious room.

A room that, just hours prior, was filled with his honorable crew.

Christopher blinked, and the horror-stricken faces of his comrades flashed across his mind. He winced at the pain again.

1

Though each glance through the viewport pained him, they also gave him a sense of relief. There was no sign of the Terran flagship that had attacked. His hearing slowly zoned in and out with his focus, allowing the distress call into his mind.

"This is the First Captain of the Homage division," his voice rang over the PA system, *"calling for immediate rescue and retaliation. We are in a critical state. Our coordinates are Seventeen-hotel..."* It continued on before repeating, but for Christopher, it felt like a constant ringing.

He flicked his fingers along the surface of the data table, keying commands for the array of sensors throughout the ship. Most of the sensors flashed offline, but those that remained painted a heartbreaking picture.

Life signs dropped all across the ship. Those that remained likely didn't have long. His crew was dying. Old friends, new recruits. Everyone on the ship was doomed to meet their creator, and he could do nothing to save them all, if any.

Christopher flicked his gaze to the door. A titanium alloy slab sealed tight and separating him from the previous dangers, the only exit in the room.

Ideas drove through the roads of his mind. He could go through the ship and find an unused escape pod, launching himself to the first nearest Homage colony with a tailing beacon. Waiting for backup sounded like his best bet, but that increased the possibility of returning Terran forces.

Keeping one hand on the data table, he slowly writhed his left hand into the pants pocket of his red Captain's uniform. The soft material slid across his hand as he sought comfort from the object inside. An object that he found to be missing.

"What the hell?" he whispered to himself frantically. He pulled out his pockets, only to find each one as empty as the last.

His breath caught in his throat. *Where could it be?* Closing his eyes, he thought back. His memories rolled in reverse, through the ambush.

The vaporizations, explosions, and projectiles. The screams.

Christopher struck his fist to his chest, the following thump echoing through the empty command deck. *Don't think about the crew. Detach, focus.*

He thought back further, to more than twelve hours earlier, just before the attack.

He could see himself sitting at the desk in his quarters. There it was! Just inches from his hand. Then the attack began.

Christopher watched as he jumped to his feet, a siren blaring through the corridors. He rushed from the room, leaving his life sitting on the desk.

"Damn!" He cursed to himself. The pain subdued in his chest, replaced with a spark. That spark quickly spread through his veins, fire engulfing his soul.

The door beckoned him now. On the surface, he knew he had to go out and get it. Beneath the fact of his personal connection, the object represented a large security risk. In any other hands but his, it would cause chaos on a galactic scale.

However, going through the doorway had the potential to be severe. There could easily be nothing but an icy vacuum awaiting him, something that would take him months – perhaps even years – to recover from.

But that didn't matter. Better he suffers than the stability of the universe.

He glanced once more to the data table, watching as life signs continued to drop by the second. The sensor for the hallway beyond the door read offline, much to his dismay. He had no way of knowing what lay ahead of him.

Stepping away from the data table, Christopher took cautious steps toward the door. The metal frame was sealed as tightly as possible. No amount of natural human force could make it budge. He activated the control panel, glad to see it spark to life. First entering three separate security codes into the keypad, he placed his hand on the holopad, allowing it to flash-scan his hand.

Mechanisms groaned into action in the walls. Thirty seconds passed before the door began to slide.

A slight hiss emanated from the edge of the frame. Christopher's eyes widened, sweat dripping from his brow as he felt a rush through his nerves.

The door stalled before continuing, the force beyond beginning to suck at the air pressure behind him. Christopher gasped a large amount of air and leapt through the threshold, allowing the force to carry him through.

He dug his fingers into the left side of the door frame, swinging himself to the side and clutching a nearby handgrip. He watched as chairs, controls and monitors flew past him and into the darkness beyond. A little way further, he fidgeted with another control panel, waiting patiently for the lights.

They flicked on soon after the decompression ceased. Christopher let out his breath, happy to find that the corridor wasn't completely devoid of air. However, the artificial gravity and temperature control had been shut off.

I need to hurry, he thought. He turned his head and looked back into the command deck, freezing as he took in the sight.

It was torn to shreds, wires sprawled, and objects strewn about, many of which were now floating serenely in the corridor beyond. The grip on the handlebar tightened as he swore under his breath. He had built this ship in her memory, and now, it too was dead.

He shook his head to focus. Lingering on the past would get him nowhere.

Another distant hiss caught his attention. He turned to follow the sound, tracking it to a window in the center of the hallway on the opposite wall. The midpoint of the window bore a long, thin crack, the sight of which sent shivers down his spine.

The pane was likely fragile. As long as nothing touched it, it would hold.

Christopher began scaling along the wall like a spider, careful to push objects away from the window. The wall was cold to the touch and frosted over, leaving it broken and lifeless. The silver metal was tainted, bullet holes, crystalized blood, and scorch marks bathed along the deck.

The scars of war.

When working with the architects of the *Caroline*, Christopher requested to have his quarters constructed down the same hallway as the command deck, which served some use during emergencies and combat.

Combat that stemmed from his choices.

Christopher jumped as he felt the ship jolt beneath his hands. The metal structure was far too cold, and his hands felt as though they were frozen solid. A temperature like this would severely cripple a man, if that man were lucky enough to live. *Did something just hit the ship?*

The coast was clear for the time being, so he'd have enough time to check. With the command center ripped apart and most of the sensors destroyed, Christopher would have to get his own visual.

He placed his feet against the wall and gently pushed off toward the window. Any harder, and he would hit the window too firmly and release the remaining pressure, defeating his purpose.

At the rate he was moving, it would take him a minute to reach the target.

He glanced through the window, the view condensed to only a distant planet with a belt of asteroids. The planet was red, much like Mars and few other colonies in the Homage division. This one reminded him of Cleave: the origin of the war.

When the first Terran ship invaded the planet, it was met with a swift resistance from the citizens. A desperate attempt approved by the newly appointed President of Terra – Dr. Joseph Simeon – to expand and quell the looming problem of overpopulation in his division.

Caroline shook more violently beneath Christopher, just before he caught himself below the window frame.

 With his face inches from the glass, his line of sight was much wider. Peering through the clear thin barrier, his eyes only confirmed what thoughts his mind had conjured. His ship was caught, wrenched as if by some gravitational mass.

Looking through the upper left corner, he could barely make out the shape of another space vessel. From his distance, he could only see few, small details. He could scarcely discern the letters NE on the hull.

His heart rate jumped in pace as he caught onto the danger of the situation. Judging from the distance between the two vessels, he predicted contact to be made within five minutes. He began moving quicker than before. His muscles worked hard across the wall, closer yet to his destination.

The metal felt colder against his hands as his body flexed with heat. If he held on for too long, his hands would no longer be useful. Even that would take him a long time to heal.

Christopher reached the end of the corridor in what he felt was record time. He pushed off the wall to the other side, grabbing the door panel to his quarters and booting it up. As it did so, he checked his gold seventeenth century pocket watch.

Two and a half minutes to contact.

The panel was on. He pulled out his military Proof of Ident and swiped it across. Hearing a faint beep and click, he grasped the doorframe and struck it with his feet. The door was scarred mercilessly, scorched and shot to hell. If the Terrans hadn't given up, they'd have gotten inside in no time.

Without thinking, Christopher swung his weightless body into the small room, crashing into the bed frame. Pulling himself together, he gently pushed off to his desk. He hurriedly scanned the flat surface for the device he had forgotten. *Nobody had gotten in*, he thought. *It can't have gone far.*

He searched frantically in his panicked state, but to no avail. Just before he could decide on a more destructive approach to the problem, he caught the light reflecting off of something from the corner of his eye.

Under the bed. Keeping on hand on the bolted desk, he reached back as far as he could and grabbed hold of the object.

He looked in his hand and sighed with relief. It was still in near-perfect condition, disregarding the many scratches on its surface. It was centuries old, and he was surprised to have kept it so well.

A technology almost impossible to come by, yet his favorite to use. Christopher took hold of the USB drive and stuffed it securely in his pocket. On that drive was the most dangerous information in the physical universe.

It was his personal history. From his birth to the many experiments he conducted, and the location of his and the Homage governments most classified secrets. Almost nine hundred years of information.

The ship lurched, jerking him roughly against the bedpost. The other vessel must have been preparing to link to the wreckage.

He looked at his watch again: thirty seconds. Cursing under his breath, he yanked open the bottom drawer of his desk. He reached in and produced a revolver.

"Now or never," he whispered hoarsely to himself.

Twenty seconds now. He threw himself off the desk and back into the corridor beyond the doorway. Once out, he kicked off another doorway, flinging himself back in the direction of the command deck. He dragged his hand across the wall, screeching to a stop in the middle of the hallway.

Carefully, he lifted the handgun to eye level, pointing it at the fractured window. If he shot it out, the remaining air pressure would be released, and everything inside would be swallowed by vacuum, himself included.

His muscles stiffened in the cold. He was running out of energy fast.

He reflected for a second more. What did it matter anymore? There was almost 400 years of conflict on his shoulders. Most living beings would have forgiven and forgotten. But nobody had his mission and responsibility.

Now he needed to put that on hold. Time to look at the future.

Christopher took one more look around his ship. He was going to miss *Caroline*. She had found a way into his heart through the years all over again.

First Captain Christopher Brennan looked to the window, steadied the gun, and pulled the trigger.

1

3rd August 2753 09:17:23

50 years later...

The United States of America once represented the hopes and dreams of the human race. Manifest Destiny, the gold rush. The future of planet Earth.

That was 700 years ago. Now, there were no countries, no nations or states. There was only the Earth, its Council, and the Homage military.

And it was currently being invaded. On the grave of the great U.S.A., one of the most important engagements in the greatest war in human history took shape.

The assault spanned over the entire surface of the planet. Earth's forces were spread thin between the land, seas, and skies, while Homage warships defended the heavens beyond the atmosphere. A small Terran fleet managed to punch through the orbital defenses.

The end of the war was approaching, and the Council was crippling, exhausting much of the resources they possessed.

In the graveyards of the broken U.S., on the fields of the former state of Texas, the corpses of thousands of soldiers lay scattered across the blood-soaked battlefield. The air was thick with the souls of the dead, the wind carrying their haunting screams. Through the thick fog, two figures stood amongst the plains.

Chris spat out a wad of blood as he squared up to his adversary. In front of him was a Terran Bio-warrior, genetically manipulated to be the strongest beings in Human Space. The monstrosity was about eight feet tall and packed with muscle. These warriors were nearly impossible to overthrow in a one-on-one, and rightly so, Chris was having a tough time taking him down.

He tossed his Burst Rifle to the ground as it clicked empty, unsheathing his Carved Marksmen Knife. The warrior smiled eerily in response and took a swing at Chris.

Chris ducked beneath it, slashing his knife in the direction of the Terran. Before it could make contact with flesh, a fist slammed against Chris' left temple, knocking him back three feet. The knife slipped from his hand, dropping to the ground a meter away.

He recovered and shot his right fist towards the Bio-warriors face, missing by inches as the monster jabbed Chris in the gut. Chris coughed up blood and staggered backwards. He spat again and took a deep breath, allowing a second for the pain to subside.

Dashing forward, he dodged another swing from the beast and took a shot at his adversaries' throat. The Terran's neck snapped loudly, and Chris watched as his opponent's corpse crippled to the ground, lifeless.

Chris nearly collapsed, lowering his head between his legs and breathing deeply, attempting to calm his rapid heart rate.

"Holy shit," he sighed to himself.

He looked around the seemingly endless battlefield, assessing the situation he now found himself in. His smooth voice lingered in the thick air, rippling along the wind. The corpses of allies and enemies alike were spread out across the wide-open Texas plains. Chris was observing the scene when he became acutely aware of the haunting silence.

He was alone.

Other than the bodies lying about his feet, nobody was left standing on the battlefield. *Where's the rest of my team?* he thought. He had been so preoccupied with the frenzy of battle; he hadn't kept a tab on his group. Looking to the communicator on his wrist, he could see that all lights were green, indicating that no one had been lost. Despite this knowledge, he still frantically searched the crowd of the dead for any familiar faces. He needed to make sure.

The team had faced worse situations that the battle of Texas and wouldn't have just abandoned him.

"Chris Brennan to the rest of UEASF Fireteam Alpha," he spoke into the communicator. "Fireteam Alpha, please respond." He waited for a minute before repeating the message. Still, there was no response.

Chris picked up his knife and decided to stroll, finding no other options until contact was established. The battlefield stretched for miles in every direction. His team could be anywhere within that range. He walked a minute through the endless maze of corpses and debris, straining his eyes to see through the dust layered winds.

His heart felt like the air around him: thick with regret and sympathy. The weight of the battle was taking its toll.

If there was one thing about Chris that he made sure to keep to himself, it was that he regretted every kill. Though he possessed exponential combat skills, they were the last thing he wanted to use during his life. The only reason he had joined the fight three years prior was to help end the war. He felt it was his responsibility.

As a member of the United Earth Association Special Forces, he could fulfill that goal.

The soldiers who were dying – and had died during the 4 Cent War – were people. People who had lives and families, ideals to defend to the bitter end.

Chris only wished he had the memory to relate.

A bright flash expanded in the distance, blinding him for a moment. He shielded his eyes, looking up to see a large cloud of smoke and fire. More fighting?

Something hadn't seemed right about the blast. It looked as though it were chopped in half horizontally. Soon, the shockwave swept over him, and the ground began to crumble apart.

An earthquake? There were no earthquakes in Texas.

The ground beneath his feet began to shatter like glass. Chris attempted to leap to safety as it fell through, grasping for the open space just meters away, but the edge slipped from his fingers. The ground fell apart, pulling him with it.

He watched as boulders, bodies, and debris fell with him at greater velocities. He reached for the wall, his heart pounding frantically in his ears as he desperately tried to grasp anything to stop his fall. As he stretched, a quick snap sounded from his waist. He screamed as all feeling left his body.

Chris felt a very dull thud, and his eyesight blinked out.

#

Chris took in a sharp breath as he woke up in his bed. His head was pounding, begging for him to rest. He turned over, his mind relentlessly trying to pull him back into a deep slumber. He was about to do so before he realized where he was.

He threw the covers from his body and sat up on the bed. Just doing so put him on the edge of a blackout. It appeared his body was still in shock from whatever collision had befallen him after the ground collapsed.

Struggling to stand, he wobbled to the door and grabbed the handle. He yanked it open, the light beyond blinding him. His body ached as he leaned against the doorframe. His hands felt broken, ligaments likely torn and joints dislocated, but it didn't matter. He felt an ardent desire to find out what had happened.

After giving his eyes time to adjust, he looked toward the kitchen and froze. Someone was there.

His mind still tugged him to sleep as he looked her over. The woman appeared to be around his age, likely 23 if judged by appearance alone. Her hair reached to her shoulders, its dirty blonde contrasting her pale skin almost gorgeously. The plain black and white dress she donned reached below her knees.

But nothing about her compared to her eyes. They were a gorgeous red, like flares burning on the surface of the sun.

She looked familiar, but he couldn't place a name, or a history. That terrified him.

Just thinking about it made his brain sting. He flinched at every pulse, as though his blood was pumping needles into his brain. It was as if his whole existence was in pain, his whole life in the material plane.

His eyes were clenched shut and his breathing was harsh. He made no attempt to stay silent.

"Hey Christopher!" a smooth, womanly voice said excitedly. "I've missed you." His eyes shot open as he looked back towards the table.

She was standing now, just three meters from him, one hand gripping the edge. Her bare feet patted on the cold tiles as she turned to him.

How did she know his full name? He'd only introduced himself as Chris to anyone he'd met in the past four years, ever since he had woken up from his coma. He knew full well his name wasn't Chris; it was the only real he could remember. But since he had been labeled a "John Doe", that's what he offered. In all legal records, his name was Chris Brennan. Nobody knew his full name.

"Are you okay? You seem to be in a lot of pain." She sounded so comfortable around him, so caring and confident.

Who the hell was she? "I guess you're not used to this place anymore. I haven't seen you in years…"

"How the hell did I get here?" he demanded.

"The same way you always have," she said calmly. The confusion on his face must've told her something different. "W-wait," she stuttered. "You mean you don't remember me, or any of this?"

Her face was filled with concern, eyes blazing as they welled up with tears. Perhaps he was being too harsh on her. What did she mean, 'remember'? What had he forgotten?

Chris was about to respond, when a sharp pain pierced his head. Everything flashed a vivid white, and he promptly shut his eyes tight. The pounding hit worse than before, his whole body spasming with each pulse. Scenes began playing against his eyelids. He didn't recognize anything, or anyone. Voices were laughing, crying, screaming.

"Christopher!" he heard again from the mysterious woman. Her voice blended with the others. He was dizzy, everything overwhelming him. Trying to take a step forward, he collapsed to the floor, his whole body writhing in pain. The world was confusing him. Or was the world confused? He couldn't tell.

#

Chris woke with a jolt, his entire body sore from the abrupt landing. He sat up slowly, waiting a minute for the pain to subside. The sun was shining intensely above his head through the large hole in the ceiling.

He checked his watch, astounded to find the antique glass face still intact, the silver hands ticking like new. It had been half an hour.

Moving the dust and rocks off him, he slowly climbed to his feet, grunting through the aching muscles. His body was exhausted, a lot of the pain centered at his waist.

He looked up, attempting to find a route back to the surface. The wall was about 30 meters, perhaps more. It was a wonder he had survived.

On the root of a deep Sebastian Oak, something hanging caught Chris' attention. He reached for his belt to grab his glasses, only to find it was missing from his waist. His belt must've caught on the root during the fall.

He winced as he remembered the painful snap on his waist before he landed. *Damn*, he thought, *it just had to be that*. The root was five meters above the ground, much too far to reasonably climb.

Bending over, he scooped up the sharpest pebbles he could find and placed them in his left hand.

He needed to get his belt down. That equipment wasn't cheap, and some of those personal items were irreplaceable.

Chris stared up at the root, loosely holding one of the pebbles in his right hand. He stood as still as his sore body could handle, determining the angle at which he would need to toss the small stones.

After a few seconds, he cocked his arm back and flung the pebble through the air as hard as he could. He watched as a split second later, the section of rock wall directly next to the root shattered. It exploded upon impact, a crater the size of a tortoise taking its place.

Dammit. He took the second pebble in his right hand and cocked his arm back again. He glared at the root and shot the pebble.

Chris heard a thunderous snap, looking up to see his belt drop expeditiously to the ground like a ton of weights. It clanked against the rocks, coming to a halt just five meters away.

Sauntering over to retrieve his belongings, he stopped dead in his tracks as he heard another explosion. The cave walls trembled, rocks breaking off and dropping to the ground. Chris braced himself, preparing for another quake. The rumbling hadn't come from above, but seemed to emanate from deeper in the cave system.

When the trembling stopped, he clipped the belt back around his waist.

Chris noticed a large tunnel carved into the wall to his left, likely from an Obrision earthworm. He approached it carefully, tuning his ears to pick up sounds from deeper within.

War had plagued humanity for countless millennia. Men and women, fighting one another for things such as belief and self-interest, or even just for the fun of it. War had evolved dramatically over the course of existence. Weapons and styles of warfare and strategy were constantly changing.

There was only one characteristic that seemed constant throughout the course of history: the sounds. No matter where or when one goes, war can always be identified by the same resonance. The screams of the participants and victims as they were struck down, the thudding of their now lifeless flesh crippling to the foundation of the skirmish. The searing of swords, battle axes, bullets and lasers slicing through the air, the whispers of death lingering all around. At least, that's how Chris had taught himself to perceive it.

That was exactly what he heard at the end of the tunnel.

"Where the hell did Chris go?" a familiar voice queried. He jumped when he heard it.

It had been Katherine's voice, there was no mistaking it. He heard some faint crackling, and remembered the comms device on his wrist. Another voice came through, this one male.

"Chris, d'you read? Shout out if you receive this."

Chris clicked the feed button on the device, bringing it closer to his face. "James, this is Chris," he spoke with a sigh of relief, "I read you loud and clear. Where are you guys?"

He waited a moment for a response, listening intently to the static coming through. Though to his disappointment, nothing did.

"James," he spoke again, "anyone, do you read me?" He was desperate now. After all this time, he had just found his friends. At least he was relieved that they were alive.

Looking back down to the wrist comms, he noticed that the microphone had been damaged. *Seriously.*

He hadn't been abandoned after the battle, it had just moved on without him. It must've been pure luck that he had found the new stage. Nearly an hour had passed since he began searching for everyone.

Of course, he had to assume that his friends were the ones at the end of the Obrision tunnel. It was entirely possible that a different group of Homage soldiers were fighting. Either possibility, there was only one way to find out.

Chris moved into the opening of the tunnel, his tall frame scarcely fitting. He was around six feet in height, so this was not an easy task. As he waddled through, the war song grew louder.

At around the halfway point, another explosion occurred, this one much fiercer than the others. The force of the blast jolted the entire tunnel, making its walls unstable.

Various sections behind him began to collapse. Chris hurried his way through, struggling to make it to the end without being crushed by tons of rocks.

Before the remaining length fell through, he leapt out of the tunnel, falling a meter to the ground.

Looking up, he found himself staring into the shocked face of another Terran Bio-warrior.

The two men stood for a moment, staring in shock at the sudden presence of an opponent. Chris reacted as fast as he could, briskly drawing his Carved Marksmen Knife from his belt.

He rushed at his new opponent, moving the honed blade towards his throat. Just before it cut, however, the warrior dodged, swinging his fist into Chris' abdomen. The force of the impact flung him back into the cavern wall, causing the weapon to fall out of his hand.

As Chris slowly recovered, the Terran threw another punch to his face. Having dodged by mere centimeters, he watched as the warrior's arm went through the wall with incredible force and speed.

Chris leapt away and looked back to see the Terran struggling to pull his arm out of the wall. It was stuck, as if by some sort of powerful adhesive. Seizing this opportunity, Chris picked up the CMK, increasing the length of the blade, and swung it towards his attacker.

In one quick swipe to the forearm, the Terran fell away from the wall. He looked at the stub just below his elbow, blood rushing from it and splattering onto the stone floor.

Eyes back up to Chris, the Terran made eye contact just in time to see him take another swing.

Chris watched as his opponent froze with a shocked look on his face, his final breath cut short, as if the menacing warrior had turned to stone. As another, smaller explosion from a grenade went off nearby, the Terrans body fell backwards, his head falling off his shoulders and rolling down the rocks.

With that small scuffle having ended, Chris finally found the time to observe the scene he had injected into. Just from a glance, he could tell it was brutal. Though nowhere near as gross as what he had left, the floor was littered with crimson-stained corpses, with many more soldiers fighting amongst them. From where he stood, the only living soldiers he could see were average Terran forces, wearing their traditional type 27 Combat Armor.

Chris respected them in that sense. They stuck with tradition. In 400 years, they had managed to maintain a sense of culture and camaraderie throughout the series of warfare. Among them were the less traditional Bio-warriors, though they made up far less of the mass.

He counted about fifty soldiers in all.

The platoon of death was rioting against the far wall of the football field length cavern, with bodies flying, dropping left and right of the main point of focus.

Lucky for Chris, the mass of soldiers hadn't noticed his entrance. That alone gave him a slight advantage.

He pivoted his body objectively towards the battle, thrusting himself into a full-on sprint. The element of surprise was always an influential factor in warfare, and can often turn the tide of any battle.

If the Terrans were to attack him head on, even he might not be able to survive. Those Bio-warriors were designed to be deadlier than the vacuum of space.

His plan worked out well enough. By the time he had arrived at the edge of the crowd, it was too late for any who noticed to react.

He grabbed a helmetless Terran soldier by the hair. Reaching around with the CMK, he slit the mans throat and shoved the corpse onto two other unsuspecting soldiers, knocking them to the ground.

As Chris attacked, it was as if time slowed down. His heart was pounding harder than usual, which he found odd. Although the crowd was soon aware of his presence, the bodies kept falling. He made use of any weapon he could get his hands on.

When he made it to the center of the crowd, he felt a sharp pain sting above his hip.

Chris collapsed to the ground, writhing in pain. Looking down, he could see his combat suit had been pierced by some sort of metal projectile, bullet or otherwise. His blood flowed out, a large puddle of crimson beginning to form beneath him.

He put a hand on the wound to apply pressure as he tried to slide away from the oncoming storm of Terran vengeance. The pain was unbearable. He looked up once more to see a Bio stride towards him.

Chris began to panic. This Bio-warrior seemed more menacing than the rest. He had an ominous darkness about him.

The large beast grabbed Chris by the throat, picking him up off the ground. Chris could feel the air get caught in his throat, his life slowly squeezing out.

His vision started to blur, and he could barely make out the evil smirk of the man before him.

The monster spewed out some assumedly vulgar remarks in a language Chris could not understand, and he felt as his body became weightless.

It was then that the Terran dropped him, the warriors face blown open. Blood splattered Chris' face as he landed hard on his knees, falling onto his back. He sucked in a large gasp of air as his vision returned and he glanced up.

He sighed with relief as his eyes locked onto his teammates. James hurried to him, a med-kit in his hand. Kneeling next to Chris, James handed him a pistol. Chris began to fire at the Terran swarm as the rest of his team set up a defensive perimeter around their exhausted teammate.

Lucross stood in front of him, wielding a D-23 Dual Rifle, while Amabel, Samantha, and Katherine flanked to cover around him. James swiftly wrapped bandages around Chris' abdomen, making sure they were tight enough to hold pressure.

"Thanks," Chris said aloud for his teammates to hear. "Why didn't you tell me you'd left?"

"Things got a little rough on our part," James responded, standing back up after having finished dressing the wound. "We figured you'd be able t'finish up top while we pushed on." James held his hand out to Chris, who gladly took it.

Being hoisted up to his feet, Chris looked back around at his team.

"Well, in that case," he said, grabbing an A-22 Terran Assault Rifle lying near him. He turned off the safety and let the bullets fly.

#

The SnapShot rocked through the warm, southwest air. The ventilation system worked to disperse the heat and cool the crew down.

There was a knock at the door as Lucross let himself in. Chris was on his bunk, lightheaded and recuperating from the shot he had taken.

He looked up at Lucross, whose dirty black and white hair stood out from his tan skin and dark combat suit, which he sported with an odd elegance. A fresh bruise adorned his right eye, and he was covered in scratches. Just looking at him, it was no surprise that he was chosen as Commander of Fireteam Alpha.

"Brennan," he greeted Chris, leaning against Chris' desk. "Feeling any better?"

"Much," Chris grinned faintly, sitting up to be more level with Lucross.

"That was one hell of a shot. Saw it pierce right through your combat suit. We all made it out with cuts and bruises, but nothing like what you got."

"Yeah, it was the one thing I didn't see coming. But I'm fine, we both know I've had worse."

"Well, we just finished passing over the ruins of San Francisco," Lucross stood. "It shouldn't be long before we're back on Easter Island. The medical personnel there could take a better look at you. If you need it, that is."

Chris chuckled. "We'll see what happens."

At this, Lucross let himself out. Chris laid back, left alone with his thoughts.

He was a little peeved that the team had moved on without him during the skirmish. They seemed to have a lot more faith in him than he did himself.

His mind wandered over the events of the day when an image flashed in his mind.

The woman in the dress, from his dream. Once Chris had woken up and reengaged the Terran forces, he had completely forgotten the dream in the cavern.

Dreams were an oddity. They had plagued every human being throughout history. Everyone had weird dreams, and they were almost always undecipherable. Chris had his fair share of odd and questionable dreams, but none as confusing – as realistic – as this.

He hoped, if given enough time to think, he could figure out the meaning. Someone in the universe was bound to know his full name. Perhaps someone from his previous life?

It was possible the dream could have been a generalization of his past. Something before the incident. Deep in the back of his mind, there was a familiarity towards her. "Why didn't she try to find me?" he whispered to himself.

The way she had spoken to him bothered him the most. Not the tone of her voice, but the clarity of her words. It was too clear, as though she were speaking directly into his mind. He could hear her. It wasn't his imagination.

A painful fuzziness flooded his brain, similar to the pain in his dream. Whatever memory his mind wanted to show him, didn't want to come through.

Chris' stomach growled. He looked at his watch to see the hour hand strike eight, about eleven hours after he fell down the cavern.

He stood slowly, his headache fading with each second. Tossing on a plain white shirt, he walked out the door and scanned the deck for everyone else.

James was sitting in the pilot seat, still in his combat suit as he navigated them to the Homage base on Easter Island. He made sure to take a jagged route, so the SnapShot couldn't be traced by Terran scouts. Lucross sat in the joint social/briefing center, tossing a data chip as he listened to something in an earpiece. Amabel sat beside him, glancing at him every few seconds. Chris could almost see the tension between them. Samantha – James' wife – seemed to be in their quarters, light shining around the edge of the door.

The lights in the mess room were on, which could only mean that Katherine was inside. Walking through the entryway, Chris observed Katherine as she kept her green eyes glued to the book in her hands. Her auburn hair was pulled into a bun, the remaining bangs brushed out of her face.

Chris tossed together a sandwich any professional would spit at. He sat two seats down from Katherine. Glancing to her, he now noticed that she was looking at him.

"Hello," she said, folding her book and turning to him.

"Hey Kat," he responded before taking a bite from his sandwich. Swallowing, he asked, "what are you reading?"

"*The Divine Comedy*," she said, looking at the cover. "It's an old copy, passed down through the family."

"By Dante Alighieri?"

"Yes." She stood, taking the book in her hands as Chris took another bite. "Chris…" she said softly, "do you think the war will end soon?"

She had asked him the question plenty of times, typically after a heavy day of combat. He tried to never give her a straight answer. Nobody knew when it would end. It had already raged for 400 years, and perhaps it could last for another few centuries. This time, however, he had an answer.

"Yes," he said, trying to avoid eye contact. "The war will end very soon. I can feel it."

It was his honest answer.

"Really? Thank God. I'm tired of all this fighting, whether it's my job or not." She sighed a tender breath of relief.

"So am I."

"Thank you, Chris. You're the best." She pulled him into a tight hug.

Releasing her, she strode from the room with more of a hop in her step.

"You're welcome." At least he didn't break her spirit.

He was more than sure the war would end in the near future. The division that will win, however, wasn't the news he wanted to break to her. The Terran force had pinned most Homage vessels to the Sol system. Other forces were spread across the division, but from his understanding, they wouldn't make it in time to help. The fates seemed to be set in stone.

It was odd that she continued to ask him such a question. His view of the world was far less significant than those of his teammates.

He was only 28 years old, while she was almost 100, and the others were well past that mark. They only looked so young from an age reducing drug administered at birth. This drug also had some diverse psychological affects, keeping their personalities younger as well.

Chris only had three years of combat experience, and four years among the world of war.

"Would y'all mind coming t'the flight console, please?" James' voice spoke through the internal comms network.

Taking another large bite from his sandwich, he stood up and threw the rest in the disposal. Walking back through the mess entrance, he wandered to the controls where James was seated. The rest of the team was already there.

James seemed to be in an odd place, though. Somewhere between burning anxiousness and calming excitement.

"So," he began, "I just received a series of messages from the Council base. They have called what they claim t'be the 'most crucial meeting of the war.' It's going to be held in 4 days in Old New York."

"Okay, so? What does that have to do with us?" Katherine quarried.

"We're not part of the Council," Lucross said, "and we've never been invited to any meetings. It shouldn't concern us until the meeting ends, so we can receive our orders."

"Well consider this our first team invitation," James corrected.

He rotated one of the monitors in front of him, presenting the messages to the group, with one chunk of bold text standing out to everyone.

The message invited them to the meeting as honored guests. Chris' eyes pulled to the sentence that stated, "ARRIVAL IS MANDATORY."

"That's an order," Chris observed. "What do they need us for?"

"No idea. It didn't say anywhere what the topic of discussion will be, but it must be pretty damn important." James moved the monitor back in place. "That's all I have to tell you guys. We'll arrive at Easter Island in about half an hour."

James turned back around in his seat. The gang broke up, going about their individual tasks.

Chris strode back to his room, his mind heavy with thoughts and concerns of his own.

He knew where he recognized the woman from.

2

4th August 2753 04:51:28

The central hub for all Homage operations, Easter Island was filled to the brim with the remaining fragments of the military.

Officers darted through the long, narrow hallways, juggling their focus between meetings and personal matters. Almost nobody had time to themselves. The base was in a state of panic after the Terran invasion, squads marching about to secure the perimeter.

Many returned from the field, while twice more were preparing to leave and attempt to escape a doomed fate.

For the UEASF, there were smaller responsibilities. Due to the hundreds of high-risk missions they are deployed on, their tasks were kept minimal at bases. They took attempts to help train volunteers, and even volunteered to assist others when possible.

After Chris and the others drove the Terran force from the surface, the base had actually relaxed for a time. But the threats were far from gone.

Fireteam Alpha received separate quarters from the others soldiers so they could keep out of the way during stressed times. Chris, Amabel, and Samantha relaxed in the social center of the quarters. The latter two were chatting about plans for the future, and their previous lives, while Chris had a small computer propped in his lap. Lucross and Katherine had already gone to the mess hall for breakfast, and James was still fast asleep.

Chris typed away, searching the Homage databases for any hint to his true identity. If he could find any links to his past, perhaps he could find her. The woman from his dream.

That wasn't the only place he knew her from, however. During their trip to the base, a memory had flashed across his mind. The only memory he could recall from before the coma: running around with a young girl in the forest as a child.

The only connection between the two were her eyes. They were a crackling red, a hue that was extremely rare in the galaxy, even among various alien species.

She was fully grown in the dream, likely meaning he had known her in more recent years.

Chris had been burrowing through the Homage medical database for some time. The list of coma patients and incidents was thousands of pages in length, even when narrowed to recent dates on Earth.

The galaxy was a large entity, and the Homage division took up a good third of it. In that, trillions upon trillions of people have been living for centuries. That much documentation was difficult to handle, and more difficult to explore. Many planets had shoddy records, especially during wartime.

"What are your plans for today?" he heard Amabel ask.

"Huh?" he noised, struggling to take his attention away from the screen. She was sitting to his right, liking watching him focus. "Probably just research," he said, looking up to meet the gaze of the two. "Why?"

"Curiosity. You've really kept to yourself since we got back to base, more so than usual."

"Well," he said with a slight chuckle, "I've had a lot on my mind."

"What are you researching?"

"Myself."

"Finally!" Samantha piped. "So you've finally decided to listen to us. We want to know, too, you know. Though it'll likely boost that otherwise angelic ego of yours." Chris watched her speak, only just realizing that the two had cleaned up. It made them look quite different. More relaxed, baggy clothes. Samantha had her dark hair down, covering half of her face.

"I'm getting to it. Recent events have got me thinking, and I'd like to know how I fit into the world, though, it's not as easy as I thought it would be."

"I imagine it to be pretty difficult," Amabel said, taking a sip from some tea.

"Likely impossible," Samantha agreed.

"I'm starting to think so, too," Chris admitted, sighing.

The door to James' bunkroom opened slowly, the man staggering out with glazed eyes. He maneuvered around the edge of the couch and plopped next to his wife, letting out an elongated yawn.

"Are we going to get breakfast or what?" he asked, running his hand through his messy, bleached hair.

"Well hello, Mister 'I need at least four hours of sleep to function'," Samantha chided to her husband.

"Funny." James jokingly tossed a crumpled paper at her, which she swatted at, laughing. "So again, breakfast?"

"I guess. I'm sure we're all hungry." Samantha and the others stood, Chris closing his computer and following. "Luc and Kat went ahead of us."

They walked into the outside corridor, where dozens of soldiers were dashing about. A man was leaning against the wall to the left of the silver door. He was wearing a very unusual uniform. It was yellow, and held elements of a high-ranking officer, but other pins that Chris didn't recognize. Perhaps he was a liaison to one of the colonies? He stood straight when they walked out, fixing himself up as he approached.

"Hello," he quickly greeted them, his voice smooth, foreign, and professional. "My name is Alex Subarr. Would any of you happen to be a Mister Lucross Stone?"

"No," James answered, annoyed. "He's out at breakfast, which is where we're trying to go."

"What exactly do you need him for?" Amabel asked, defensively.

"He hasn't done anything wrong," Subarr explained, "if that's what you're asking." He was taken aback by the aggressiveness of the team. "I just have some urgent matters to discuss with him." He paused for a second. "Classified matters, from the Council."

"Like we said, he's not here."

Alex was too professional for Chris to read. There was no fault in his actions or words. None that Chris could catch, anyway. And that's what bothered him. Chris hated professionals.

"No worries. Do you mind if I accompany you to the mess hall?"

"Feel free," Chris said. The team looked to each other, their faces asking too many questions.

Exactly what I was hoping for today, Chris sighed. As they neared the door, Lucross walked out, catching them off guard. Looking at Alex, his expression grew a bit serious, but his eyes seemed to lighten a bit.

"Mr. Subarr, it's nice to finally meet you in person," he said as he neared them, extending his hand to the stranger.

"Likewise, Commander Stone." Alex accepted the gesture, taking Lucross' hand firmly. They locked eyes, some sort of information silently being liaised between them. It was as if they were communicating telepathically. "If you'll excuse us for a while," he said without bothering to look at them.

"I'll see you later," Lucross said to Amabel in a near whisper, taking her hand in his. He brought it up to his mouth, giving it a gentle kiss.

Never before had any individual member of the team been called for classified business, despite their rank. It was all or none in most cases. Then again, the war was coming to a swift close. Not everything would be as it was before.

Lots of decisions needed to be made, and not everyone was going to know about them. Maybe that's what happened with Lucross.

Chris walked through the doorway and into the mess hall. He scanned the crowd of faces to find Katherine sitting motionless by herself. She had her book in her hands, emerald eyes wide as she read. Chris grabbed a plate of fruit and made his way to her table, sitting in the seat to her left.

"Hey," he said, a smile on his face. Perhaps his happiness could cheer up a hopeful person like her.

"Hi Chris," she laughed. "Nice of you to join me." She seemed surprised by the sudden appearance of her friends, but she relaxed. She didn't like to be alone. "What took so long?"

"We got held up," Chris said before digging in.

#

He shouldn't have waited so long. Four years held too much turmoil and chaos, and now there was no real way for him to discover anything about his history.

Chris had spent hours sifting through medical records dated around the time he had gone comatose. There was nothing to give him a new lead, the only thing possible relating to him being an incident report filed two years before he woke up. Though the type of incident wasn't specified.

Other than that, there was nothing. Even his own medical files held no information about it, only his injuries:

deflated lungs, ebullism, anoxia. Apparently his incident wasn't as important as the starships, asteroids and planets burning all throughout space.

In the years Chris spent making a new life, he had never considered the old one.

Chris had taken his awakening as an opportunity. Even now, he wasn't a fan of the past, and always looked to move forward. How many people had he abandoned up his awakening? He had given up on them without a second thought.

Laying back on his uncomfortably soft bed, he let out a long sigh. He was tired. Every time he put thought into the dream and memories, it put stress on his brain on top of the anxiety of wartime.

The dream, the woman who may or may not be a childhood friend, his ordeal in the cavern, getting shot. So much had happened in such a short amount of time.

Is this really the life I was meant to live? He already had the combat experience of a war veteran, yet he was still in his prime, not even a sixth of Lucross' age.

Chris sat up slowly, careful not to rattle his head too much. He pulled off his shirt, grabbing hold of the bandages around his waist. As gently as he could, he unwrapped them.

The bullet wound had healed completely. Less than 24 hours: a new record. His body was odd that way. It was extremely durable, and any damage done, no matter how devastating, healed within 48 hours. As long as it wasn't lethal, that is. He'd had his fair share of near death experiences, and hoped never to knock on that door again.

He unhurriedly laid back down, rolling onto his side. Breathing in deeply, a cool burn developed inside his chest. The Council meeting was in two days, and there was no knowing if he felt excitement or anxiety.

Supposedly, the meeting would focus on the impending "Cessation" – what the Homage populations had christened the end of the war. Chris, however, drew a blank on that purpose. What more was there to say about it? They were losing, out of options. Nothing the Homage force could utilize to end the 4 Cent in victory. *We're doomed for failure. That much is obvious.*

Chris sat up and slipped back into his shirt. When the meeting would conclude, free time would be scarce. No time to research, no leads to follow. No time to relax. Chris stood up and proceeded to exit the barracks. He left his communicator on, in case anyone else decided he was needed.

The base stretched the entire length of the island and dug beneath over a mile deep. Chris was three floors from the bottom.

He walked through the maze of corridors, finding himself at a set of seven elevators. They seemed to be in minimal use, Chris managing to get the center lift all to himself.

Before the doors closed, he caught sight of Lucross and Alex Subarr walking in his direction. Chris couldn't quite hear what they were discussing, but it was something about an assignment. When they noticed him staring blankly at them, they stopped and waited for his elevator to leave.

The doors slid shut, and Chris leaned back against the wall, staring at their silvery shine. *Odd.*

The lift began to rise, velocity increasing as it shot him toward the surface. It would only be a minute before he arrived.

Just as he got comfortable against the railing, the elevator shuddered to a stop after 63 floors. It jerked him around, igniting an ache in his body.

The doors slid open, and Chris was greeted by a gorgeous, starlit sky. The moon shone bright overhead, bathing him in its full light as he stepped out of the lift. He stood still, observing the landscape. The ancient moai stood scattered across the hillsides, moonlight adding to their mysterious grace.

Chris stared up at the stars. Nothing pleased him more than to see the beautiful balls of plasma shining bright above his head. Through the polluted air, the depth of space only magnified their brilliance. It was rare that Chris could find the time to admire those diamonds. No matter what happened to humanity Chris found comfort knowing that the universe would always shine bright.

There was always a hope for something far greater. That was when the stars seemed to be the most brilliant.

"Gorgeous, isn't it?" Katherine's voice flowed. Chris looked over his shoulder to find her leaning against one of the ancient statues. "I never come out here often enough. But when I do, I always find myself looking up."

"I was thinking the same thing," he said, gazing back up at the deep sky. The sight put him in a trance, and for just a second, he let everything go. Something about it made him feel warm, as if he were looking towards home.

Katherine sauntered over next to him, sitting herself on the soft grass and looking up at him. She snapped at him, pulling him back down to reality.

"Join me?" She patted the grassy spot next to her. He smiled in response, dropping to the ground and laying back. The grass felt soft under his fingers, like the fur of a husky.

Katherines eyes seemed to capture the magnificence of the universe, as if galaxies were born in her soul. She had a relaxed smile on her face, and her effulgence flooded the space around them, a feeling of comfort hanging in the air.

It almost broke Chris' heart.

A loud ding emanated from the elevator. The doors opened slowly, revealing the rest of their team.

"Mind if we join?" James asked, giving Chris a smirk. Chris returned the gesture.

"You're more than welcome," he said.

James and Samantha fell next to Chris, taking up a similar position as Samantha laid her head on James' shoulder. Amabel and Lucross took up the back, fingers interlocked with one another. The whole group, together as they should be, admired the beauty of the night sky.

Three hours passed before they returned to their quarters to sleep.

As Chris laid back in his bed and slithered under the covers, he fell asleep with a smile on his face.

#

New York had once been such a grand city. One of the busiest in the United States, and a land to pursue one's dream.

Now it was rubble and dust.

Buildings had been blown to pieces, many toppled or reduced to ash. Fires spread, dotting along the streets and walkways. The once busy streets were barren, no sign of life in sight. Chris was glad to be far above, so as not to see the littered bodies. The thousands of corpses...

In the back of his mind, he still searched for leads, but the light of that mission grew dim. He had waited too long. The woman from his dream would likely remain a mystery, and Chris had to accept that. Define his future, not his past.

The SnapShot began to shudder, slowing from the coursing speed they'd travelled for three hours. The Council meetinghouse was supposedly nearby.

Chris hoped to get inside as soon as possible. He wanted to put the unsightly graveyard behind him.

Standing, he walked to James, who was focused on steering the craft. Chris put a hand on his shoulder and looking through the viewport. James always had the best views from the pilot seat.

"Are we about there?" Chris asked.

"Seven more miles," James responded plainly. "I hope this meeting will be good." He didn't sound too excited to meet the Council, likely under the circumstances. His tone was almost akin to sarcasm or grief.

"I'm sure it will be. Why would they call us in just to remind us that we're losing?" A question Chris wanted answered for himself as well.

"True." James kept his eyes forward.

Chris smirked nervously to himself. Everyone on the ship was full grown, some centuries old, yet they acted like anxious teens. He couldn't help but feel that he and Lucross were the most mature of the bunch. The team was diverse, but perfectly blended.

He turned and moved to his seat in the briefing area. *This meeting is going to be painful.* Still, something about the situation changed for him. His surroundings seemed to brighten. The overall tone of the world changed.

It'll be alright, something said in the back of his mind.

It was a very smooth sound, and he had an easy time trusting it.

Soon, the ship slugged to a full stop, hovering thousands of meters above the ruins. James was trying to stay out of sight of any remaining Terran drones.

"We're at the coordinates," James announced over the ship comms.

Chris looked through the window, scanning their surroundings. The city had grown over the millennium since its founding, with no end to its sprawling streets in sight.

The ground beneath the ship began to split open, bringing up the unpleasant memories of Texas. It continued for ten seconds before stopping. The hole was at least half a mile in diameter and pitch black.

Lucross entered the deck from his room, coming to a stop behind James.

"Take us down, Knight," he ordered James. "They're expecting us. That hole is one of many entrances." James gave him a confused look, likely unaware as to how Lucross held that knowledge. "Hurry up. We wait any longer and someone is likely to see us."

"Yessir," James said hesitantly. There seemed to be some mistrust, though it likely only stemmed from the surrounding anxiety. Lucross was their Commander for a reason. Intellect, bravery, combat skill; he had been a role model to Chris when he joined, as well as other soldiers throughout the force.

The ship hummed softly as it descended into the pit. It passed between the gray and black charred buildings, the walls surrounding them and climbing higher. They were soon swallowed up by the shadows.

The ceiling above began to slide shut, the lights inside shining brighter as it progressed. Interior lighting now at full capacity, Chris could see that they had descended into a large underground hangar, which was nearly empty. Most ships were likely used for evacuation during the Terran invasion. The SnapShot came to a halt in the center air space of the large room.

"There," Lucross pointed at one of the many vacant docks, which lit green a moment after. James pitched the flight controls forward until the SnapShot hung above the spot. He gently lowered it onto the scratched metal surface before turning the engines off.

"What now?" Katherine asked as she entered with Amabel and Samantha behind her.

"We standby for a representative to escort us in."

"Let's at least wait outside of the ship," Amabel suggested.

"I suppose," Lucross agreed thoughtfully. "As long as nobody wanders off."

Unsure of what to bring, Chris stuffed a small notebook into his belt next to his USB drive and moved in behind the group.

The bay was a lot larger than Chris had anticipated, as he expected the Council base to be more similar to the renovated Capitol Building. The hangar itself was at least thirty stories in depth, walls dotted with empty docks and control centers.

Only seventeen of the likely hundred or so spots were in use. Everything was metal and alloy, ranging from stunning silvers to deep blues and everything in-between. Tubes and wires ran along the floor and ceilings, with holopads standing at each docking space. Very bare bones compared to the Easter Island complex.

Twenty minutes passed before a representative strode through the nearest door. His bald head radiated the light, and he wore a very crisp Council uniform.

"Hello Fireteam Alpha," he greeted upon arrival. "My name is Pansh Stents. I hope your flight was enjoyable?" He paused for a second and looked among them, almost as uneasy as they were. "If you will all please come with me, and have your Proof of Ident ready for each checkpoint."

They followed Pansh through the doorway and into a maze of hallways. The walls were painted a lovely maroon, though the paint was peeling in several areas. Lights flickered now and again, and everything held a very ancient design.

At the end of the third passageway, they passed through another door. A red sensor scanned each person as they walked through, searching for weapons or synthetic disguises.

Another entryway produced a panel, where each member was to present their POI, provide a hand scan, and receive a once-over by facial recognition software. A very slow process, considering a DNA scan would be much quicker and more secure.

Every team member passed through and descended a flight of stairs. Chris glanced at the walls, assuming there were automated defenses hidden throughout.

They hit the bottom of the stairwell, silence intensifying as they moved further from the surface. The air was thick and stale, circulation kept to a minimum between the stairwell and chamber doors.

The doors were large, a lot more modern than the rest of the facility They gleamed, lines of blue light pulsing across the surface. The Council chamber, Pansh informed them, was just through the threshold.

Pansh Stents pressed a small button and the thick slabs of metal slid apart.

Chris was stunned as the cool air swayed over the team. The chamber was enormous, granite pillars lining the circular wall. It was grander than Chris could have imagined. There were 54 elevated seats of silver, two for each Homage colony. Almost each seat was filled, representatives busy at work.

A section of wooden seats were kept in the center of the room for the team, where they sat gingerly.

The member closest to them, the First Councilor, stood to address his new company.

"Rise," he spoke. The team snapped to attention, keeping as still as possible. "Come forward please." His voice was booming, though he didn't raise his voice. It echoed through the chamber, and caused an ache in the back of Chris' mind.

The man wasn't just powerful in position, but in stature and spirit as well. He was dressed in the most formal and decorated uniform Chris had ever seen in his career, which hugged his seemingly muscular body. On his chest was a tag that read "Alterous", obviously his name. A powerful name to fit a man with a powerful aura.

He wouldn't take his eyes off Chris.

The team approached the tall podiums cautiously, Lucross leading the pack with pride. They stopped a foot away. First Councilor Alterous handed Lucross a tablet filled with text.

"Each of you scan your thumbprint. It will act as your signature. This document is a pledge of silence of this location, and contents of the brief discussion that will take place. If any of you refuse to sign, you will be dismissed immediately and have your short-term memory wiped. Clear?"

A resounding "yes sir" resounded from them before they passed the tablet around. Chris was the last to scan before handing it back, the team moving back to their seats.

Chris sat in the back left most seat, James and Samantha next to him. Katherine, Amabel and Lucross planted in the front row. They all looked to Alterous, who was now also sitting.

"Now with the formalities out of the way, let us get to business." The way the man shifted from formal and commanding to casual and calm was unnerving. Two ends of a spectrum should never meet like that, especially in a man so powerful. "We have been at war for hundreds of years. The Terra division is showing no sign of slowing. We're almost out of resources to focus on efforts from Earth, and aid cannot be received from the other colonies for another two months. We have taken many extreme measures, as I am sure you are aware."

"Yes sir," Chris was surprised to hear himself speak. The room grew silent as everyone turned to look at him. He looked up at Alterous, who was staring intently at Chris.

"There is one final measure we have yet to take," he continued. The team was motionless, mouths agape with shock and confusion. They had witness weapons and prototype tech from the history of Homage weapons research and development used over many years. Most of those had devastating effects, and Chris was surprised they were even *considered* for use. *What else could there be?*

"The Council has argued about this last resort for many months now. Some of our members even abandoned us when the bill had passed for its creation. After many years, I have decided that, in order to defeat the Terran threat, we have no other choice. We considered including you all in the discussions, but politics are not your field of business."

"Sir, what is the measure?" Amabel asked, head tilted in confusion. "Like you said, we've exhausted everything, correct?"

"Correct. There are no classified weapons left for use. However, this last measure is not a weapon, nor was it intended for this kind of use. A project from almost two hundred years ago, headed by our Lead Scientist. Very few people remember its existence, myself included. We abandoned it fifty years ago after an incident at its location. Everyone we could save was evacuated and we left it in the dust.

"At this time we cannot tell you what it is, nor what it is capable of. All I can say is that it might just win us the war, but we need you to procure it."

"So," Lucross spoke up, "you want to send us on a mission to retrieve something dangerous without any implication of what it does?"

"We are not asking. It is an order, Commander."

"Luc," Katherine interjected, "if this is the only chance for us to end this conflict, wouldn't you want to take it?"

"She's right," Amabel agreed. "You've told me hundreds of times that you'd do anything to end the 4 Cent, to end the suffering on top."

There was a silence. Everyone waited for an argument from Lucross, but nothing came. His face scrunched up, contemplating his options.

"Where's the device, Councilman?" James asked. "It would need t'be very isolated t'be kept such a secret."

"It is," Alterous confirmed. "Any of you heard of Minkowski Two-dash-Nine?"

"The Twin Jet nebula?" Chris quipped. His love of the stars was rooted deep, and this certain planetary nebula was one of his favorite celestial structures. The Twin Jet nebula, also lesser known as the Cosmic Butterfly, was one of the most beautiful natural formations he had ever seen, as if crafted by the hands of an angel.

"Precisely. We developed a large science station nearby, based on the results of the first test of the device in its experimental stage. The base was constructed to mask said effects."

"Sir, that body is twenty-one-hundred lightyears away. It'll take us quite a while to get there and back."

"We have developed a new Hyperdrive. One that travels faster than any craft has ever experienced before. We can push the Terran force back and hold them off long enough for your return. We need this, Christopher." *What?*

"I'm all for it," Chris stuttered out, caught off guard by the use of his full name. "But it's not up to me." He turned to look at Lucross.

It was Lucross' responsibility to accept missions for the team. Despite team discussion and agreement, he was the representative Commander.

"Yes," he said without warning. "We'll do it. When do you want us to leave?"

"One week, but we need you to report to Pan immediately." Alterous sounded pleased. He glanced across the faces of everyone in the group, lingering a bit more on Chris and Lucross.

"Yes sir."

"Then you are all dismissed. Good luck. You will need it."

They all stood, saluting as they turned away from the Council and traced back out the door with Pansh. Chris could feel the eyes following them out. But this time, it made him more than excited.

He'll finally see the Cosmic Butterfly in person. Other than the old scientists from the base there, he was going to be the first human being to see it up close.

This is gonna be one hell of a mission.

Before he forgot, he pulled Pansh Stents aside to ask him a question.

3
15th August 2753 17:18:42

Stars had always influenced the culture of mankind, dating back to the beginning of their evolution.

Primitive civilizations would look into the night sky and craft theories and theologies to make sense of it all. Everything above their own little world.

Those masses of hydrogen never ceased to amaze, not even to the most advanced species, and Chris could see why.

Space travel had always been one of his favorite aspects of enlisting in the Homage military. More often than not, his team needed to travel through the vacuum for long periods of time. Though being in space raised his anxiety, nothing beat seeing the universe with his own eyes.

One week passed after the Council meeting – though it was more like a glorified mission call than meeting. The whole discussion only lasted about ten minutes total.

Short in nature, it had much greater influence than any other mission during their careers. They had been called in by the most powerful people in the galaxy and given a cryptic mission: a very rare – and very big – deal.

The mystery of it thrilled Chris.

Hours after the meeting, they had travelled to the Homage colony of Pan. At the mountain base on the biggest continent on the planet, Donish, the SnapShot was taken to be fitted with the new Hyperdrive. This new drive was purported to have a top speed of 30,000 times the speed of light in Hyperspace.

The team had been ordered to prep for the week they spent on the planet. The base was nearly abandoned, and it almost always rained outside.

The day of their departure, there was no place Chris would rather be. The SnapShot sailed more smoothly than ever before. Alpha team was just reaching the edge of the solar system, preparing to switch on the newly attached Hyperdrive.

Chris watched through the rear window at the large star as it decreased in size with the expanding distance. He stifled a yawn, eyelids getting heavy.

He was tired, but there was no way he was going to miss the new drive in action.

Hyperspace had always been a tough concept to experience. In a few cases, it had driven people to madness, the passing universe scrolling through their heads a million times over until their brains fried. For others, it was the most pleasurable experience they could imagine.

Chris was part of the latter demographic. However, travelling 6.59 billion kilometers per second? Nobody knew what it could be like at the velocity. The numbers were tough to wrap his head around.

A sharp jolt sent Chris sliding across his bed. Recovering, he looked back towards the window.

The stars and planets he had admired were gone, barely enough time to glimpse them before they slipped from existence. Instead, they were replaced with a dark pitch he had never seen. In Hyperspace, they travelled so much faster than light that it was practically invisible. If viewed from outside, the SnapShot would look like a single shining entity in a black void. Just looking through the viewport gave him a headache.

Next to that feeling was another, calming sensation. *This is the closest I'll ever get to home.* A thought he didn't feel consciously.

After a minute, an odd luminescence could be glimpsed for brief moments at a time.

"This is surreal," James' voice crackled through Chris' wrist comm. Samantha could be heard in the background, mumbling something inaudible.

"It kinda hurts to look at," Katherine added, a hint of nervous excitement in her voice. *"It's putting a lot of strain on my eyes."*

"Same here. Y'all should rest, we've been up a while. Sleep could be a very good medicine."

Not in this case.

"How long will the trip be?" Chris spoke into the mic. He knew the math; travelling 2100 light-years at 6.59 billion kilometers per second.

"Thirty-five days, give or take."

Over a month on the ship. Granted, it usually takes longer to travel such distances at the decreased hyper-velocity he's used to, but even so, this was going to be a very long journey if he had to keep staring into a void.

If they used the Hyperdrive only, they'd have enough fuel for the trip and then some. The drive ran off photons, just as any other model, as well as components that weren't disclosed to his team, except for maybe Lucross.

"Alright then," he sighed. He plopped down onto his bed. "Wake me in a few hours, I guess."

"*Goodnight Angel,*" a familiar voice came through. As he heard it, his mind switched off, and he was asleep.

#

Chris' mind snapped awake, his name called from someplace distant. It sounded as though the voice was ringing in his eardrums. He sat up quickly, shaking his head.

The voice didn't stop calling, emanating from somewhere off in the ship. He reached over and switched on his stereo, pressing the volume up as high as it could go. He wanted to drown it out, to be left alone. Whatever was in his mind, he had no intention of listening.

After five minutes of Bach, the voice faded. Whoever needed him had now given up. *If they need me, they'll fetch for me in person.*

Chris stood, almost losing his balance with the hangover of his headache. He staggered sleepily to the sink next to his desk, filled a cup with water and took a large gulp. His mouth felt like the Sahara Desert.

"I'm losing my mind," he mumbled, looking at himself in the mirror. The blue in his eyes seemed to have grown a purple tint. He squeezed his eyes shut, and once he opened them, the tint was gone. He couldn't help but notice the streaks of gray in his hair were still in place, though barely visible. The stress had affected him in more ways than mentally.

His hair was a mess, greasy and standing on end.

Grabbing a towel, he walked out of his room and to the vacant locker room.

Nobody else seemed to be around, but Chris caught a glimpse of somebody turning the corner to the mess room, likely Amabel based on the dirty blonde hair.

He entered the restroom shower stall, locking the door behind him. He turned a handle and hot water began spraying onto the tile flooring, steam rising into the air.

He sighed as the miracle liquid ran down his torso. Whenever he got the chance to swim, he would imagine himself floating through the beautiful breath of the universe. He stood still as the water fell on his shoulders, trickling down his spine and treading the back of his thighs.

Something tickled the back of his mind. A form of memory, trying to be pulled back to life.

It hurt. Whatever it was, it was hurting him. His world was spinning left and right, and he had no idea how to regain control.

Chris finished up his shower, running his towel lazily over his body and wrapping it around his waist. He yawned loudly, body still exhausted.

As he stepped through the doorway, his foot caught on the bottom of his towel. His eyes widened as the metal floor briskly approached his face.

He sat up as quick as he fell, breath caught in his throat in anticipation. His eyes darted around. He was back in his bed. Wires were stuck to his temples, extending to a life monitor.

What the hell?

Yanking the wires off him, he threw his sheets onto the floor and stood. He put on a shirt and pants before walking hastily through to his door. It slid open quickly as he exited.

The rest of the team was standing in the middle of the main deck, left of the briefing center. They were talking low to one another. Katherine must've heard his door open, because she looked up just in time to see him stride out.

Her eyes widened, and she sprinted over to meet him. She threw her arms tightly around his neck, embracing him as if he'd been gone for years.

"Oh my God, Chris!" she cried out. "I was so worried, are you okay?" *Worried? What for?*

"I'm fine," he said slowly, very confused. *How long was I unconscious?* "Just a bump on the head, nothing to fret over." Hearing this, she backed away, allowing him room to breathe.

"What do you mean a bump on the head?" Lucross asked as he approached Chris. "We found you in your bed three days ago. You wouldn't wake up at all."

"No. The last thing I remember was hitting my head outside of the locker room."

"Chris," Samantha interjected, "after we jumped into Hyperspace, we didn't hear from you for hours. Katherine went in to check on you, but you wouldn't wake up."

"I did everything I could to wake you," Katherine supported.

"We figured the safest thing to do was to leave you in bed, so we brought the equipment to you."

Chris stayed silent for a few seconds, their words passing in one ear and out the other with no understanding.

"Chris," James said considerately.

"Amabel," he interrupted, looking to her, "you were there. I saw you walking into the mess room. It was only a glimpse, but it had to be you."

"I haven't been in the mess room," the tone of her voice scared him a little. "Luc brings us both our food."

"We monitored yer brainwaves while you were out," James continued.

"You were thinking," Lucross finished for him. "A lot. Your brainwaves were literally off the charts. I've never seen anything like it in all my years. Whatever you think happened was nothing more than a dream."

"Then why does my head hurt?" Chris asked defensively as his brain throbbed.

"With all that brain function, my head would hurt, too."

"I've heard of cases similar to this all across the galaxy," Samantha piped, "impacted long-term coma patients. Has this ever happened to you before?"

Instead of answering, Chris found himself tired of the nonsense his friends were spewing. He turned around, walking back into his quarters and locking the door behind him.

#

For the next week, Chris spent most of his time looking through the window.

The darkness intrigued him, no longer putting a strain on his eyes. It was interesting to watch space as it was before the Big Bang, before light and sound.

He made sure to document it, snapping photos and reading from the ship for future study by the scientists of the Homage division.

Chris believed in a lot of things. The Big Bang, multiverse theory, and more. The way history had taught him: there was never only one of anything. Lifeforms, planets, stars, galaxies; there was always an abundance.

He hoped that one day he could pioneer an expedition for something gargantuan. Just the thought excited him, to be the first man in a new universe. If such a thing existed, a lot of humanity's problems would be gone. No fighting for space due to overpopulation. Though, that likely wouldn't come to fruition for many millennia.

27 days after their departure from Pan, Chris was reading through incident reports from around the time he had fallen into his coma – more out of interest in others than himself. Katherine entered the room with James and Samantha. He hadn't noticed their entrance at first, until Katherine placed a hand on his shoulder.

"How are you holding up?" she asked, a hint of concern in her eyes.

"What? I'm fine. You don't need to worry about me."

"You almost never come out," Samantha said.

"You only come out for food and showers," James specified. "You're givin' us every reason t'worry."

"I don't think that's accurate," Chris argued. "I just needed some time to myself for a while, to figure things out."

"And?"

"I'm good now, I promise. Nothing can take me down for long, you know that. And Tyler can eat his words."

There was a silence. Everyone looked uneasily at Chris, and then at one another.

"Um," Katherine began, trying to formulate the question in her head. "Chris, who is Tyler?"

"A man I knew long ago. He helped me through a rough situation, to which I was grateful. Good guy, haven't seen him in years. He predicted that I'd never get through every obstacle in my way, but now and again I have proven that wrong."

"He's part of the military?"

"No, way before my military career."

"You told us you don't remember anything from your past," Samantha said.

"I don't," Chris paused.

I remember something.

"Then how d'you know about Tyler?" James asked, intrigued.

"I guess it just dawned on me," he trailed off.

"Tell us more," Katherine pressed.

"Okay, well," he thought hard, "I was in a bit of trouble. I don't remember where, but something had gone wrong. I think a malfunction of some sort. Anyway, I was making my way to evacuate, but the last shuttle had taken off before I arrived." Where is all this coming from? "Just when I thought I was left for dead, out came Tyler. He pulled me into his ship and took me out of the danger zone."

"What was Tyler like?" Samantha interrupted.

"He was a lot like me. Tall, athletic build. Great sense of style. Hazel eyes, brown hair. He was an average, good looking guy."

I remember something!

"Chris, what was his last name?" Katherine asked hopefully, bouncing twice on her feet. "If we could find him, maybe he could tell us more about your past."

"His last name?" Chris focused, trying to dig further into his newly found memory. "Damn, what was it? I don't remember much, only what he was like. I don't remember asking for it, or if he just didn't give it to me. I don't think he was supposed to be there."

"Damn," Katherine sat on his desk, disappointed.

"What about where this all took place?" James asked, his full attention on Chris. Chris' friends had always wanted to learn more about his mysterious past, so they were fully invested in this conversation. To them, it was like listening to a legend.

"Some sort of station? I think. I don't know, it's a blur." He was so close to remembering. He could feel it, but it was slipping away. "Just forget it, okay? Whoever he was, or where we met, it was too long ago. It's a lost cause."

"Well, alright. But now we need t'make sure. Are you okay?"

"That's the whole reason we came in here," Samantha affirmed him.

Chris smiled. Something he hadn't done in days. He was glad to have friends to support him, even if they couldn't do much.

Life had been getting quite strange, and he loathed it. Dreams, familiarities and the sudden rush of ancient memories. This was all the reason he never wanted to explore his past. It always had the possibility of damaging him, psychologically. Look forward, never back.

"I'm perfectly fine," he finally said. He stood and gave each friend a quick hug, leaving Katherine with the longest. She was more worried and supportive than James, and Chris had known him the longest.

The others left, and Chris sat back at his desk, contemplating his reality.

#

On the 35th day, James began decreasing the terminal velocity of the SnapShot by small margins.

Their destination was closing in, and Chris found a beat of excitement in his heart.

He was about to witness the Cosmic Butterfly firsthand, his favorite natural structure. Pictures had been taken from telescopes and satellites, but very few were taken up close. It would be a completely unique experience.

"Everyone report to the briefing area, please," Lucross called over the static-filled internal comms.

Chris hurried out and sat in his seat promptly, everyone else taking their places around him. The arrangement was almost identical to that in the Council chamber. Lucross stood by the two meter screen, combat suit zipped and remote in hand.

"Alright," Lucross began, "the Council gave us a series of files to read over before we arrive at the base." He paused after the word, his face scrunched in thought. "I read them over just three hours ago, so I'll save you the trouble of the uninteresting details." He clicked the central button on the remote, and an image of the Twin Jet nebula materialized onto the screen.

It was subtly different from the old pictures Chris had seen in astronomy books. The red and green colors were fading, and it was a lot larger.

"This is where we are currently headed: Minkowski two-dash-nine, a bipolar nebula spanning light-years in length. Our target, however, is down here." *Click.* The image zoomed into the bottom left corner, where a dark planetary shape could be seen. "This is the planet we are currently hurtling towards. The Lead Scientist designated it Ljuska, and it's home to the most classified experiments and information stored by the Council of Earth. No details of those experiments were provided to us, so we're flying blind to whatever dangers could be inside."

Chris watched every movement Lucross made, like it was a performance.

"After the incident we were informed of, an energy shield was activated over the surface to keep anyone from getting in, or anything from getting out. According to the documents, these shields were made to be 'impervious to any known measure of force at the time of construction.' We're required to find a way inside."

"Were any terrain details included in the documents?" Chris asked. "What about the condition of the planet?"

"The condition is unknown. Supposedly nothing on the world could be accessed remotely, likely for security reasons. But in fifty years, either a lot has changed, or nothing has." The answer didn't satisfy Chris, but it was all he would get. "Does anyone have ideas on how to get past the shield?"

"Are any of our weapons strong enough to take it down?" James asked, thinking of a forceful approach.

"I doubt it. Our current weapon models were still in use at the time, so the shield should hold under that pressure."

Chris gazed out towards the nearest window and into the void beyond, zoning out as the others thought up more suggestions.

"Wait." *I have an idea. Holy Hell, I have an idea.* Chris found an odd confidence in himself. It was the best and craziest idea he ever had. "The Hyperdrive," he spat out.

Such a good plan.

"What about it?"

"It's the only technology on the ship that wasn't in use during that period of the war, right? If we attach it to some sort of large, durable object, and send it off at top speed –

assuming the shield is as powerful as they claim – then the shield would shatter. The impact would also slow the drive to a decent fall, preventing any real, lasting damage to the planet."

"Wouldn't the impact eliminate the drive?" Amabel asked.

"Not if the drive has the same effect on the object as it does the SnapShot. Otherwise, we'd have disintegrated the second we switched it on."

"Not too bad of an idea," Lucross noted.

"You're right," James agreed. Chris looked at everyone, an unexpected look of surprise on their faces.

"Okay," Lucross continued. "We need to find the heaviest object on the ship that we'd be willing to sacrifice. While you work on that, I'll dig through the documents to find the exact durability of the shield. Brennan: crunch the numbers. Make sure everything would work according to *your* plan."

"Yes sir," Chris beamed.

4

19th September 2753 06:20:59

The numbers checked out, according to the programs Chris had run.

The provided Council documents listed the maximum strength of the shield to be 4.490 quadrillion Newtons. The plan, then, was to attach the drive to a motorbike in the bay of the SnapShot and send it off at top speed, assuming it all held together. The impact would force the shield to faze out, and the drive would be slowed to an easy fall to the surface of the planet.

Damage and retrieval were impossible to predict.

In the bay, Chris was working to attach the Hyperdrive to the small vehicle, Katherine and Samantha standing behind him. He could feel their eyes, only adding to the pressure to not mess up.

With the prominent level of raw power packed into the machine, it was more than likely unstable. He needed to be careful, or he could destroy himself and the rest of the ship. As he finished torching the final inch, he noticed that his hand was shaking.

"This is going to be interesting to watch," he said as he stood, turning off the torch.

"Exciting, to say the least," Samantha agreed. "James said we're almost slow enough to see everything."

"Good."

"Of course you're excited," Katherine said jokingly. He wasn't trying to hide it very much.

"How could you tell?" he chuckled, winking at her.

Chris was glad to be in a much better mood, the atmosphere of the unorthodox mission flowing into his mind. Acceleration far faster than the speed of light, a world lying outside of two dying celestial masses. Not to mention the mystery of what lies on the surface of said planet. Chris felt he was living the most far out adventure in history.

"Let's get this bird moving, then," he slapped the drive before they left the cargo bay. It was going to be a bumpy ride.

"Hey!" Lucross' voice sailed from the pilot area. "We've dropped from Hyperspace. Come take a look." He sounded fascinated, which concerned Chris. Lucross was rarely impressed.

Chris hurried his way to the bow of the SnapShot, moving swiftly past the rest of the team.

"Holy shit..." someone said behind him. A state of awe spread among them. Chris couldn't move.

The mass spread across the entire viewport. The stars in the center were locked in orbit, dying as they shot material into the two spiraling solar jets on either side. It spread so far, they couldn't see the ends in either direction. The colors of the nebula were bedazzling, shades of red and green coalescing within one another while streams of blue shone through like veins in the wings of a butterfly. It was shaped almost like an hourglass, laid on its side.

"Wow," Chris said softly.

"Did y'get the Hyperdrive hooked to the bike?" James asked, forcing Chris to divert his attention from the celestial fireworks.

"Yes, I did."

"Good, because we're nearin' Ljuska. Look there." He pointed out the bottom left corner of the window, where a red planet was sleeping next to the astronomical power display.

"It's a red planet?" Amabel asked, moving closer to the window to get a better look. "It looked a lot more earthlike in the pictures."

"It is earthlike," Lucross said, wrapping his arm around her waist. "That redness you see is the shield."

"How did they manage to get that thing up?" Samantha asked.

"It's actually twice the size of Earth. They gave no details about it, just that the only way to take it down from the outside is with extreme force."

"Let's get this done," Chris stuttered suddenly. He jogged into the bay and heaved the Hyperdrive into position, facing toward the exterior door. "Go ahead and open the door," he called over the comms. James must've heard, as the door began to lower slowly. Chris took a deep breath, allowing his mind to focus.

The SnapShot came to a halt and began to rotate 180 degrees. The planet came into view, its shimmering shield flickering with pulsating power. He could barely make out the surface through the thick barrier. He aligned the drive as straight as possible.

"*Alright Brennan,*" a voice addressed him through his communicator. "*Get back up here so we can send it off. Is it aligned?*"

"Affirmative," he spoke through the tiny mic. "On my way." Chris walked fast, his wide gate getting him to the main deck in no time. He sat in the briefing area, flipping on the video screen and switching the view to the bay camera feed. The others joined him, bar James, who remained in the pilot seat. His hand hovered over the Hyperdrive activation switch.

"On yer order, Luc," James said.

"Now," Lucross ordered firmly. James flipped the switch, and a loud whine filled the air.

The screen flashed a brilliant white. Once it cleared, the Hyperdrive had disappeared. Not a millisecond later, a depression was bending into the shield.

Chris watched intently, fingers tapping on his knees as the drive dug its way into the barrier. Time seemed to slow for Chris. *If this doesn't work, we're done for.*

Just as the thought of failure flashed among his mind, the shield shattered like glass, the pieces dissipating into free energy. Just before the break, James had begun hitting more switches to deactivate the drive.

They were lucky. Any number of things could have gone wrong.

"Great, it worked," Lucross stood, growing serious. "No wasting time. We're not sure if it's a permanent shutdown. Knight, lock us down and take us in."

"Yessir," James sounded off.

"Everyone else, get yourselves ready. We're moving out as soon as we make landfall. Grab everything you need."

Chris stood up fast, his vision blurring for a moment before getting to business. In his room, he effortlessly stripped of his casual clothing and grabbed his combat suit. The texture of the crystalline cotton and armor felt great underneath his fingertips, but it irritated him when he found the bullet hole in the hip.

As he slipped his legs inside and yanked the suit up to his waist, the ship jerked violently. He was thrown to the floor, hitting his head on the bedside. *Ouch!*

"What the Hell was that?" Chris yelled into the communicator, trying to regain his composure. He began to stand, steadying himself on the bedframe when the ship was thrown again, tossing him into the wall. He looked down to see small amounts of blood piling onto the floor.

Fucking Hell! He could feel his weight lighten a bit, and the lights inside flicked out. They were falling towards the planet's surface.

While everything was relatively stable, he struggled into his suit and zipped it up. Clipping on his belt, he made his way out to the main section of the ship. Looking out the bow viewport, he could see rocky terrain falling towards them.

"Hold on!" James yelled.

Chris jumped to his seat, sitting down and strapping in as he saw James do the same. He closed his eyes as James tried to save the powerless ship.

5
19th September 2753 07:12:42

"What's the damage?" Chris faintly heard Lucross say from a few feet away.

Chris slowly opened his eyes, his sight blurry and painful. He blinked quickly and cleared his vision.

Red lights were flashing everywhere, meaning the power must have been restored. He didn't know how long he had been out.

"The thrusters were damaged extensively, as was the left wing," James listed, a diagram on the main viewscreen of the ship highlighting the damaged sections in yellow to contrast the healthy blue. "There was barely enough thrust left after I rebooted the system t'break our fall. The hull was breached in several sections when we landed, and the engine overheated."

"How long before we're able to get her back online?"

"I'd say about three hours, three and a half at the most t'fix the thrusters and breaches t'the hull. The engine will cool on its own."

Chris unhooked himself and struggled to stand up. He placed his hand on his head, where it had been hit beforehand. Pulling it away, he saw his hand was engulfed in blood.

His legs felt as though they were about to give out on him, but they continued to support as he hobbled to the restroom. He was sure there was someone calling his name, but he didn't care to pay attention. Lazily looking in the mirror, his eyes shot open.

The blood had spread from his head down over his right ear and along his neck. A vessel had burst in his left eye, the white covered in the red liquid, making him look like some sort of demon.

He grabbed a towel and put it under some water, scrubbing the blood off himself and cleaning the wound on his head thoroughly. Turning back to the sink he was in front of, he turned it on and bent his head down, splashing water into his eye. He looked back into the mirror to see that the crimson had faded.

"For now, everyone continue preparations if you have not already done so," Lucross yelled from the main deck. "If you've finished preparations, I advise you to eat something and rest a little. We've got a long trek ahead of us."

Chris walked lamely, making his way to the mess room, stopping by his room to grab a messenger bag and his laptop. When he reached the kitchen, he tossed in several different food packets. Throwing the bag over his shoulder and grabbing a drink, he sauntered back to the control area.

Everyone else was sitting patiently, as Lucross stood by the screen with a remote again. *Another briefing?*

"Alright," Lucross began as Chris dropped into his seat. "This is a map of the surface. The two points you see represent us, and our objective. It's about a twenty-three-kilometer trek to the west of our position." The map on the display wasn't very detailed, lacking any prominent features of the terrain. "Those twenty-three kilometers should take us about four hours, depending on the terrain along the way.

"Unfortunately, our exterior cameras were damaged in the fall, and the blast shields activated on the windows before collision. We have no idea what to expect before we exit the ship."

"You said it was earthlike, right?" Katherine asked.

"Fifty years is a long time for a planet to be abandoned," Chris dissected. "Any number of things could have happened, including whatever incident caused the abandonment in the first place."

"Exactly," Lucross continued. "We have to approach this with caution. The Council neglected to inform us of any dangers or details. Not to my surprise, of course. We're flying blind: no clear target or knowledge of the environment. Just a basket full of shit." Anger tweaked his voice on the last line.

"Let's go," James sighed. "The quicker we do this, the sooner we find ourselves home."

They stood, gathering supplies before moving out. Lucross snapped a long-range rifle to his back, the others armed with magnums. They made their way to the cargo bay, where James punched in a code and lowered the ramp.

It wheezed open more slowly than before. In doing so, Chris was greeted by a cool breeze flowing through the opening. He instinctively took a long, deep breath.

To his amazement, the air was the cleanest he had ever tasted, especially compared to the smog-filled skies of Earth. *So natural.* He looked back through the opening, and his eyes widened.

Thick brush dotted beneath thousands of large red, green, and blue trees. They, along with the tall grasses, swayed gently in the morning breeze. Hills rose and fell along the horizon, colors shifting from the one before it. There were more than one species of each plant type, and Chris recognized many of them being from other Homage colonies. Each one looked unique from the others around it.

Above them, clouds swam against the blue sky, flocks of birds soaring just beneath them. Some were from Earth, while others had an odd shape that Chris couldn't discern from the distance.

It was as if a rift had opened to a prehistoric Earth. A time before humanity had worked their poisonous hands into the soil.

He was bewildered, a feeling of warmth rinsing his soul with familiarity. Time would pass by seamlessly in an environment like this. People would pay millions just to step foot on this soil.

So vivid. *So synthetic.* A true masterpiece of nature.

"Let's hurry," Lucross said, snapping Chris from his wonderous gaze. Lucross seemed uncomfortable in the unique environment.

They stepped cautiously into the warm sunlight, a sharp contrast to the chill of the winds. Chris watched the clouds continue to creep by, stretching across the skyline.

"Where did the sun come from?" Chris hadn't noticed earlier. It had given him such a comfortable feeling. "This planet is stationed next to a nebula, and this side isn't even facing it. The sky should be in a perpetual state of night."

"Perhaps it's a simulation," Amabel suggested. "Projected onto the energy shield, I assume. To give whatever wildlife is living here a familiar scene."

"An odd assumption, though likely, considering people resided here for a time."

It hadn't felt different from any other world they'd visited during the war. What bothered Chris, however, were the unlikely circumstances in which Ljuska existed. It was identical in nature to Earth, with an alien flair thrown in; the sky was artificial, and its location in the universe was very deadly, let alone impossible. The planet shouldn't even breathe. Something was very wrong.

After an hour, they passed a small waterfall that descended into a nearby river. The patter of the water on the rocks and the rustling of the trees blessed their eardrums. Small fish could be seen swimming in schools beneath the surface of the water. Insects swung through the air as cute, squirrel-like creatures darted along the grass and into the trees. In the distance, towering animals could be seen faintly among the trees, a mountain range behind them to the south.

It added some ease to know that the animals were being preserved. On their home worlds, many species had perished in the war.

The trek was long for Chris. He wasn't fond of hikes through unknown territory. The temperature picked up quite a bit as noon rolled around, to his surprise. He expected a constant temperature throughout the day due to the shield protecting the planet from any natural solar heating. The scientists must have built some sort of heating and cooling center somewhere else. If it got so hot during the day in the fall, how must it feel at night?

They were about three quarters of the way when they entered a long, low valley. A field in the center produced short, blue-green grass that flowed like the smooth waters of the river they had seen long before. As they entered the field, they began to slow. The team didn't make much small talk during the trip.

"Alright," Lucross said, breathing heavily. "Let's take a quick break, this is exhausting."

"Oh, my goodness, thank you!" Katherine exclaimed as she plopped down into the tall grass. "Holy shit, it's so soft." She stretched out, sighing into a relaxed state.

The rest of the team followed her lead, sitting down on the tender grass. She was right, of course. The grass felt as soft as a thin cotton blanket.

Chris slung his bag off his shoulder, pulling out food he snagged before leaving.

The group slowly began to talk amongst one another as they regained their strength, friendly as ever. They finally adjusted to the awkward comfort of Ljuska.

"This has actually been a pretty easy mission," Samantha was saying. "Compared to most, anyway. I'm liking it."

"Same here," James agreed, grabbing hold of her hand. "Definitely beats fighting Terrans day and night."

"I really like the scenery. You can't find this anywhere in the galaxy anymore."

"This mission has been one large magic eight ball, that's for sure," Chris said. "The Council really did leave a lot of this up to chance."

"We've always had luck on our side, though," Lucross piped in. "We were lucky enough to have such a diverse team." Amabel smiled at him, wrapping her arms around him and laying her head on his shoulder.

"I'm just glad th-" Chris cut himself off as he caught sight of something sitting across the field.

The earth beneath them shuddered with a pulse as the team stood quickly up, listening intently. The vibrations reminded Chris painfully of their last mission on Earth. The thumps grew more intense as a sudden roar resonated through the clean air.

Chris looked closer at the creature. It was bipedal, standing still on its hind legs, and large, easily about six feet in height. It was bent at the waist, and he guessed about eighteen feet from head to tail. Its long arms were pulled close to its feathered body, with lengthy, clawed fingers to tip them off. Chris wanted a better look, but just as he moved, it took off sprinting in the other direction, into the trees.

"What was that…?" Katherine asked nervously. Her eyes darted around, looking for the source of the terrifying bellow.

"There's no way." Chris said. "That's impossible."

The pulses in the ground grew louder and stronger, then stopped.

That's when they spotted it. A large beast, even its softest footsteps thunderous enough to cause trees to quake in fear.

No details could be seen through the thick tree line, but the rose gold eyes piercing the shade were clear. The monster froze, and Chris could hear the snort of its nostrils, sniffing intently at the surrounding air.

That's when Chris whistled. It came as an impulse. He could see the pitch snapped its attention, so he whistled again, lower and longer. As he continuously raised and lowered the pitch, he slowly muscled away from the rest of his friends.

"Chris!" James whispered to him. "What in the hell are y'doin'?" He seemed to be angry, probably from the danger Chris was putting himself under.

"Just trust me." He looked back to the trees, watching as he slowly drew out the savage beyond. Sure enough, it slowly stepped out into the light, almost matching his own.

He took one look at it, and he couldn't look away. The beast had him terrified, fascinated.

It was huge, at least nine feet in height, and just over half as long as one of the *SnapShot's* wings. A patch of white, featherlike structures lined along its back stood out from its mottled greenish-brown scales. Eyes stared intently at him under slightly prominent ridges.

The titanic creature began to move forward, steadily keeping eye contact with Chris. He could hear it breathing, noticing that it could smell him from such a long distance. The way it cocked its head to the side as it lumbered forward…could it hear him breathing as well?

It stopped again, but the thundering in the ground continued. *There are more,* he thought. *A family?*

Chris moved with it, whistling more in lower tones. He observed the creature more as it moved to follow him cautiously, as if it were curious.

Luckily, it was ignoring the rest of his team, who were slowly making their way to the thick shelter of the trees. They had no intention of leaving him behind, he was sure of that. They knew he would have a plan of some sort.

But he didn't.

More details could be made out as it came closer. The long, serrated teeth jutting out from its narrow snout were more closely packed in the front. Its forearms were short compared to the rest of its dimensions, measuring only about as long as Chris' if fully stretched, with two short fingers.

Holy mother of…

It was a dinosaur. A living, walking, breathing dinosaur. And not just any, but the most popular prehistoric beast in Earth history, the tyrant itself.

A Tyrannosaurus rex. Standing just yards away, its massive body parallel to the ground beneath it. As it moved, a deep rumble could faintly be heard, emanating from its throat. The whole time, it just watched Chris as he moved slowly. Maybe confused as to why he wasn't running away? Smaller creatures would scurry away from such a predator, but Chris was standing his ground, calling to it. Standing before this tyrannosaur was a small beast that it had never seen before.

"Not so extinct anymore, eh?" Chris grinned nervously at it.

The T. rex opened its jaws, unleashing an earsplitting roar. It took a deep breath, and bellowed again, stomping in place a bit. Was it challenging him? Surely it would feel superior, there was no need to challenge.

Chris heard snapping off to his right, and looked to see two more tyrannosaurids, both larger than the one Chris had been interacting with.

He had been playing with the child. His friends were nowhere to be seen. His plan had succeeded, but now he was stuck.

The adults began striding forward at a slow, steady pace.

One was green, just as the juvenile, but with no feathers, and scars on its snout. It seemed at least twice the size of its child, if not more. Chris assumed this to be the male. Its companion, the supposed female, was a bit larger. Her skin was more of a reddish brown, running from darker shades to lighter from top to bottom. The ridges above her eyes weren't as prominent, with the eyes being just a bit larger than the males, and with a slightly thinner neck.

By the looks in their eyes, Chris could tell they weren't happy.

They made it over to their offspring, the mother taking the left and the father the right. They both looked over the juvenile, sniffing and nudging at it.

They turned their attention to Chris. In unison, they let out a terrifying chord of anger. It was a threat. He could tell that he had put himself in more danger than intended. Shaking uncontrollably, he turned into a sprint towards the trees.

He could hear the rexes immediately give chase, the thundering of their strides nearly causing Chris to trip. He had backed out to the center of the field with the juvenile, so it would take more effort to make it to cover.

Even if he did get to the trees, where would he go? The tyrannosaurs crashed through the towering autotrophs like they were nothing. He couldn't hide, they'd be able to sniff him right out.

Chris hurried towards the trees. As he looked up, three blurry streaks of feathers darted passed him and towards the rexes. Chris stopped and swung himself around, watching as the three man-sized creatures pounced onto the larger rex.

The rex began to twist and turn, roaring furiously as the small theropods bit and slashed at her. The male rex bellowed in defiance, but continued after Chris. He turned to run again, keeping as far as possible from the deathly scene behind him.

A deafening shot rang through the valley, and a painful shriek came from behind. Chris turned and saw that the male tyrannosaur had diverted its attention elsewhere. Following its gaze, he saw James standing at the valleys edge with a rifle in hand, smoke emanating from the end of the barrel. Unfortunately, it did nothing to hurt the monstrous beast.

Tyrannosaurus rex was physically built like a tank. Its skin was thick and durable, with a layer of fat and muscle beneath. It would take a lot more than one shot to do any real damage. They had the greatest stamina of any living animal.

The male rex began moving to James as he shot again and hurried back into the thick brush. It gave no indication of giving up, but at least stopped its rampage towards Chris.

He looked to the female, who was distracted by the charge of the smaller dinosaurs for a moment. She had managed to kill one of them, and wounded the second by clamping her hard jaws onto it and tossing it away.

Chris jogged to the edge of the trees, swinging around a thick trunk and collapsing. His breathing was hoarse, and he couldn't stop shivering. He had never been so scared in his life.

Catching movement from the corner of his eye, he watched as the younger male quickly darted into the woods, roaring profusely.

Poor thing. I'm sorry.

Another, louder shot rang out across the field. Chris circled his head around the tree to watch as the mother tyrannosaur fell to the ground, blood pouring from its neck.

She seemed to be looking back to Chris, but this time, there was no anger in her eyes. All he saw was a plea for help.

She didn't deserve it. He felt guilty, far more so than when he killed Terrans. Of course, he had never witnessed a death like this in his life. He gazed at his feet, watching them vibrate. Looking up, the buck was striding towards his dead companion. Its tail swayed from side to side as it walked, balancing with each step.

Chris looked as the rex sniffed at the corpse of its lover. He thought he could see a tear emerging from the tyrannosaurs eye, but from such a distance, Chris couldn't be sure. The buck let out a loud, emotional bellow that almost made Chris cry himself. The rex was mourning the loss of a loved one.

It seemed the rex couldn't handle any more of the little skirmish. He took another look at the doe, roared in agony, and quickly strode away to the trees, where it effectively burst through the foliage and was gone. Chris was astonished that such an enormous creature could move at such a pace.

Chris turned back to the other side of the tree, letting out a long breath as he slumped to the ground and closed his eyes. Just as he began to relax, he heard the growl, all too familiar to him now.

He opened his eyes again to see the juvenile standing just ten feet from him.

Chris couldn't move. He was petrified with fear. This had to be it. There was nothing he could do; the small tyrannosaur would catch him with ease.

The rex moved towards him, gently stepping forward. It looked over Chris, analyzing him. Gold eyes still beamed with curiosity. It was close. So close that Chris could have touched it, and felt it breathing.

Chris heard a loud screech as another one of the smaller dinosaurs ran in and tackled the larger prey, the ground shaking as they collided with it.

Now that it was up close, Chris could finally tell what species the smaller theropod was. It had a sickle claw on the middle toe of each foot about the size of Chris' hand and a narrow head with red rimmed, blue eyes. It was covered with feathers, scaling from white to brown and black, all over its body except for its ankles, feet and snout.

The creature was obviously very durable, yet lightly built for quick movement.

It was a Dakotaraptor.

The raptor and the juvenile rex fought, claws and teeth tearing the flesh of one another apart. The tyrannosaur seemed to have the advantage, due to its generous size, and wasn't large enough to be slowed by its own mass. There was screeching and roaring all over, and Chris worried it would make his ears bleed.

The little rex grabbed hold of the raptors tail between its powerful jaws, producing a loud crunch. The raptor made a high-pitched scream and proceeded to attempt to leap onto the rex's back, though it didn't succeed.

The raptor's sickle claw began to strike the rex's neck, and the poor monster bellowed in pain. The rex fell to the ground defeated, but not dead.

The raptor was just about to make the kill when it froze in its tracks and snapped its head to look at Chris.

Chris was shaking again, faced by a legendary hunter who had been evolved to kill.

He slowly moved his shivering hand over to the hilt of his CMK and grabbed it tightly. The raptor screeched at him, spreading its wings in some sort of show of dominance and intimidation. It worked. Chris was scared shitless.

Chris watched as the Dakotaraptor pounced, its wings still spread out and its eyes locked onto its new human target. Time seemed to slow as death was inching closer to him.

Chris leapt out of the way, slashing with his knife towards the raptor as one of its claws nicked his neck. He had only managed to chop a few of the feathers of its left wing. The raptor hit the tree as Chris scrambled to get onto his feet and gain some sort of leverage, but it was quicker to recover. It jumped onto Chris again, knocking him onto his back and mounting him, pinning down his arms with its powerful legs.

Chris writhed underneath it, trying his best to escape. The raptor screamed at him again, its face just an inch away. Chris froze, petrified. He could do nothing now.

As the raptor was about to latch its teeth onto his neck and rip him apart, a pair of jaws appeared and bit hard into the raptor's own nape. The tyrannosaur juvenile yanked the smaller theropod off Chris and tossed it at the tree again.

Chris could hear the raptors bones snap. It writhed on the ground at the base of the tree, trying to recover and get back on its feet. The little rex strode over and clamped its jaws onto the raptors neck again, the raptor crying out in pain. In one swift motion, the rex snapped its oppressors neck, allowing its limp corpse to collapse onto the ground.

The rex turned and fell next to Chris, motionless. He considered its eyes. It was in pain, but alive.

It must've been exhausted. It looked up at Chris, who was still scared beyond belief. *Why is it looking at me?*

The rex held a position where its slender head was a foot away from Chris. He could make out every detail about the scales on its rough skin. Its teeth were yellow and stained with blood. It wiggled one of its little arms, as if asking for something.

Chris reached out his hand carefully, mind racing but blank all at the same time. The rex growled a little, but Chris didn't stop moving. If he made one wrong move, his arm would be bit clean off.

He placed his hand onto the animals hide, feeling the rough texture of its scaly epidermis, scratching it a bit. The rex closed its eyes and made a noise that sounded distinctly like purring.

It was friendly. It might have been the whole time. Chris wished he'd known that sooner.

This was a Tyrannosaurus rex, one the most vicious carnivores in Earth's history. It should've been mauling Chris, tearing him limb from limb.

Prehistoric science wasn't near as accurate as modern science. There's a limit to what could be learned about an animal that had been extinct for 66 million years. Though it certainly wasn't anymore. How were these creatures alive, and how had they gotten to Ljuska?

Chris could hear the voices of his friends talking amongst themselves quietly some distance away. It was apparent that the rex heard it as well. It lifted its head up, looking to the source of the sounds. It wiggled its tiny arms and did its best to stand up, making haste in the opposite direction. Chris watched as it disappeared into the thick leaves of the forest.

Poor little guy.

"Chris!" Everyone hurried to him. They must've thought he had been injured, seeing the blood on the ground around him.

"Are you okay?" Katherine asked. She wrapped her arms around his neck, hugging him tight.

"I'm just fine." He pulled away from her tight grasp gently, saying, "Who fired the sniper rifle?"

"I did," Lucross held up the rifle, the barrel still steaming from its previous use.

"You could've left it crippled," Chris mumbled under his breath angrily.

"What?"

"Anyone know what those things were?" Amabel asked, looking at the deceased Dakotaraptor. "I've never seen anything like them on the other colonies."

"It's because that species is from Earth, and it's extinct. That was a dinosaur."

"A what?" Katherine queried. Did they not know what a dinosaur was? The creatures had been a big deal all between the nineteenth and twenty-third centuries back on Earth. The whole cosmic revolution must have directed more attention away from the mother planet and its history.

"Dinosaurs were large reptilian and avian creatures that roamed the Earth about 66 million years ago. Almost all of them died and had gone extinct, except for those that evolved into birds."

"Well if they're from Earth, how did they get here?"

"I'm more worried as to how they're even alive."

"Maybe it's a Jurassic sort of scenario," James said. "They were able t'reverse engineer birds, or they found some sort of genetic material and brought it here for experimentation or weaponization."

"Do you know how low of a chance there is of them finding any genetic structure from millions of years ago?"

"About as much of a chance that any of this shit happening," Lucross interrupted, sounding impatient. "We need to get moving."

"Yeah." Chris was exhausted, but he didn't have a choice. Lucross was the leader, and whether or not he wanted to admit it, they all wanted to leave as soon as possible.

Not much else happened for the last leg of their trip. The scenery was gorgeous, but the oddness of everything ruined it. Chris didn't like the artificial flavor.

What confused Chris the most was that, after all the warnings from the Council, there was no real danger anywhere.

What was the "freak accident" that supposedly occurred 50 years prior to their arrival? They wouldn't evacuate an entire planet for nothing. There was no radiation, no anthropomorphic mutations of any kind, or even threat of some astronomical phenomenon.

That's what he had expected, but there were no signs of the incident, or any presence at all. Where were the buildings? The military structures?

It couldn't be the dinosaurs. They weren't dangerous enough to warrant a shield over the planet. A whole planet, covered up for what? It didn't make sense.

Soon enough, they reached the coordinates of the supposed rectangular structure.

To their dismay, nothing was there. They stopped directly on the point from the digital map, looking around.

"What the hell?" James said, looking at the tall trees and lush grass for any sign of something unnatural, or some sort of straight line. Nature never built in straight lines.

"It's been 50 years," Lucross said, quoting himself from before. "Really think it's still here?"

"Well you can't just up and hide an entire structure. The prints you showed us in the documents were huge. Where did it go?"

Chris turned back, looking down the hill they had just hiked up.

"I think I know where the lab went," he said.

"Where?" Amabel asked.

"We're standing on it."

"And what exactly makes you think that?" Samantha snapped at him.

"We're standing on a hill, directly on top of coordinates to a secret facility the government built 300 years ago."

Samantha turned back and laid her head on James' shoulder. Chris gave him a questioning look, but the only response was a slight shrug.

"Spread out," Lucross commanded. "Try to find an entrance to something."

Chris moved out by himself, not feeling well enough to talk to anyone. He was starting to get an urge to just give up. To go home and let the war be lost.

It wasn't much like himself, and he knew it, but there was nothing else he or anyone could do. Every second Fireteam Alpha spent away was another second the Terran force drew deeper into Sols defenses. They were going to lose no matter what happened, and he just had to accept that.

He had avoided it for so long that the loss would be far more painful.

He had a feeling the others thought so, too.

He scanned around, stepping with more force in various places. He was trying to find something that felt more engineered than the other sections of rock. It was more difficult than he had thought.

After five minutes, he had not found a single sign of a man-made structure.

They had been on the planet for hours, and the only artificial thing to be found was the sky. There had been no buildings, roads, signs, or any evidence of civilization. The

Council must have lied to them. Maybe sent them away to keep the Homage dream alive? So far away that they would be safe from any sort of attack. That made more sense than anything.

"I found somethin'!" he heard James yell. Chris shifted to look in his direction, noticing a straight line in the dirt stretching from Chris' position to James and further beyond.

James was kicking at the ground, pushing the dirt and grass away with his foot. Everybody jogged over to him, watching as he uncovered some sort of metal surface, shimmering dully in the bright afternoon light.

"What is it?" Samantha asked, tapping it with her foot. It sounded hollow underneath, the waves of her taps reverberating beneath. "Think it's a door?"

"No idea. We need t'uncover it some more, come on." They all began scratching at the ground, trying to uncover as much of the structure as possible.

As Chris dug, he noticed text painted on the surface. He continued to dig faster, until the entire word was revealed unto him.

"*Response*," he read out loud.

Lucross looked at him curiously. "What?"

"The word here," Chris pointed at the red lettering. "I'm assuming it's the name of the place?"

"Could be. I was never given a name."

They kept scratching away at the dirt and rock, pulling grass by the roots until some sort of progress could be seen. It was very laborious work, a type that Chris was not used to accomplishing. He was a fighter and technician, not a gardener.

It took more than ten minutes to find the edges of the hatch. They muscled all the dirt and dying grass as far away as possible, keeping it out of their way.

Chris knelt beside the metal framework, tapping on different areas to see what responses he could get. He needed to know how advanced the technology was for him to hack it. If such proved to be fruitless, they would make a forceful attempt inside.

He tapped, two rhythmic beats after another over almost every inch of it. Chris could hear the rest of them tapping their feet and sighing. He couldn't really blame them.

It had been a long day, and this had not been a mission they were used to. All this waiting and hiking wasn't their style, and there was a reason. *Hopefully we'll be out of here soon.*

Tapping one more time, a panel slid open underneath his tired hand. It lit up, a bright teal color, the shape of a hand materializing onto the small screen.

"Well then," Chris muttered as the team knelt with him to expect it.

He pulled his glove off and carefully pressed his hand onto the dirty screen. It seemed to have aged a lot in 50 years, and Chris was surprised it wasn't warped in any way.

He sat as the panel began to glow, scanning his hand for authorization. This planet must have had some super-efficient power source for the structures and shield to continue working for so long.

The panel made a succession of beeps, and the mechanisms of the door began to grind beneath them.

It beeped again, saying in a womanly monotone voice, "*Welcome, Christopher Brennan.*" He looked at the screen, surprised at hearing his name. A picture of him flashed on to the screen for a few seconds, though it looked foreign to him.

He had longer hair, and a younger sort of look in his bright eyes. The picture disappeared as the door finished opening.

"Alright," Lucross said, "let's get in there and find this thing."

One at a time, they dropped into the dark hole, descending into the abyss below.

6
19th September 2753 12:56:19

The fall was six meters into a synthetic cavern of pitch black. Chris landed next to James and Lucross, pulling a flashlight from his belt and illuminating the new hallway.

Amabel, Katherine and Samantha dropped in soon after. Chris walked ahead, looking over the surface of the metal walls. He moved slowly through the deep, cold corridor, leaving his team by the opening. Doorways dotted along the walls, leading into rooms whose purpose he was unaware of.

Each one had a basic name, such as Lab 1, Test Room 1, etc. He looked into one, shining his light through the window on the door, but saw nothing more than lab equipment and desks.

Next to the tag for Lab 5 – halfway down the hallway – he finally came upon a control panel. He swiped his hand across it, switching the lighting on along the walls and ceiling. The blue light reflected off the matte finish of the metal, likely worn from the shine typical Homage structures held.

Lines of blue lights added a nice sense of style to the architecture. He looked back through the hall to his friends, who had begun checking each room as they walked forward.

Moving forward a bit more, Chris came upon a room labeled Main Office 1, gently pushing the old door out of the way. Lights clicked to life as he passed a sensor, and he saw a right-angle desk in the back left corner of the room, notebooks and a monitor sitting still on the wood surface. Behind the desk was the facility manager's office.

Chris strode past the desk and pushed through the next door. When the fresh set of lights flicked in the next room, Chris found all of the manager's possessions in their original places, left behind and lost to time. A dusty computer sat on the desk, the screen snapping to life with the lights.

The oak desk was covered in notebooks and stacks of documents, many of which had fallen and were strewn across the floor. Chris made sure not to step on them as he moved to the other side of the desk. Plopping into the cold chair, he rotated to face the computer screen.

The system was old, likely top of the line 50 years earlier. There would be no problem hacking into it, if it needed to be done at all. Observing the monitor, it seemed the system managed to keep the manager logged in after the facility was abandoned. Documents were lined in a randomized order. Several blue tabs were already waiting on the screen, including facility power controls, a map of the compound, and more. *This will be of some use.*

He reached into his pack and pulled out his own laptop. Connecting the two systems, he began transferring the files from one computer to the other. As they downloaded, Chris observed the map carefully.

There wasn't much to go by, as most of it was similar to the other labs he had seen. He checked the map for the second level, and the third, trying to find some sort of differentiation between them.

Scrolling into the fifth – and final – level, he noticed a large room marked on the map in a yellow-green color, with a tag that read "*Restricted: Level 7 Clearance Only*". If Chris had to guess, the device they were sent to retrieve would be there.

There was another room nearby it, highlighted in red. This rooms tag, however, read "*Restricted: Facility Manager and First Captain Only*".

The First Captain was the leader of the entire Homage warfleet, but there was a change in command around the time of the disaster on Ljuska. It seemed possible that the previous one couldn't escape and died there.

Chris continued digging through the manager's system, looking for information about Ljuska and its purpose.

He opened several documents, his eyes scanning through them for potentially valuable information. Most gave details about different experiments they had conducted in the facility; all results had already been applied to the war.

A document popped into the download feed, simply labeled Blueprints. He dragged the cursor above the name and double-clicked. It took a minute to open, so Chris looked around the office.

A picture of a middle-aged man accompanied by a woman sat on the back-left corner of the desk. The woman seemed vaguely familiar, with flowing brown hair and shining eyes of the same color. Her companion was just taller than her, with a muscular build and balding head.

Perhaps the manager had escaped the planet. It was likely Chris had seen them somewhere. They all served the same government, after all.

Chris looked up just in time to catch James poking his head through the door.

"Find anything in those other rooms?" Chris asked before James could speak.

"No, we haven't," James sighed. "You seem t'be makin' yerself comfortable. Find anythin' on that computer?"

"Yes." Chris looked back to the screen, and dropped his jaw. "Yes, I did," he said more quietly, scrolling over the diagram of the planet that he had popped up. "Come look at this."

James moved over to Chris, standing behind him and looking over his shoulder at the monitor.

"See this?" Chris asked, scrolling to a cut view of the planets blueprints. He pointed to the center of the planet.

"Wait, is that…?"

"The planet is hollow, James."

According to the diagram, the crust of the planet, supported by a super dense, lead frame, was just twice the thickness of the Earth's, approximately 10-20 kilometers.

Other than that, the core was empty, bar some structural components and pathways for engineers and observers.

There was a thick, white line down the middle of the diagram. A line of text above the planet read *"Purpose: Containment"*.

"What d'you think they were trying t'contain here?" James queried, having been reading the same section of the document as Chris.

"I think it has something to do with whatever we're here for." Chris pulled the diagram of the building back into view, and pointed to the yellow-green room. "That's probably where it's being kept."

"Alright, well, let's tell the others."

Chris moved the rest of the documents onto his computer and disconnected, walking with James to meet with everyone else.

"No, that's not possible," Amabel said after Chris and James informed their team of the shocking discovery. Chris had pulled up the schematics to show they weren't lying. "There's gravity here, and an atmosphere."

"If it weren't possible, why would there be blueprints of it?" Chris replied.

"Look, it doesn't matter," Lucross stated. "We're here on a mission, not a research expedition. Brennan, did you find anything useful?"

"Yeah," Chris said, slightly taken aback. "I found a map of the compound. What we're looking for is on the bottom floor, in one of two high security rooms."

He was disappointed. Whatever mysteries were down in the core and all over the surface of the planet would have to remain as such, only because they "had a job to do".

Chris wanted to learn more; more about why the place was built, why it was abandoned, and what it's hiding. This was his only chance. They would never need to return to Ljuska again.

They followed the map, as well as directions on the walls, down through the lower levels of the base. As suspected, the second, third, and fourth floors were all near identical to the first, with many labs used for various tests and experiments.

The lights of the fifth floor flickered on as they approached the bottom of the stairwell. They slowed their approach, moving cautiously.

They had no idea what could possibly lie beyond the doors, or in the rooms beyond. They moved through the sliding door, and looked around.

The structure of the level was like that of the ones above, except for two highlighted doors. The walls glowed with the same blue light as before, with the occasional red flashing around.

"Red door first," Lucross said. "We're not splitting up this time. Keep your eyes peeled."

Moving towards it, Katherine pulled out a small explosive to place on the sealed doorway. They didn't have the specific clearance to enter either room, even with the information the Council provided. She pressed the charge onto the panel next to the door and set it for 10 seconds.

They moved back down the hallway and into the stairwell again, where the explosion shook the structure around them with a bang.

Back into the hall, they watched as the smoke cleared.

"What do you think we'll find in there?" Samantha asked.

"Don't know," James responded bluntly.

The smoke dispersed, and they could see that the door had been forced open by the blast. They moved forward in a single file line lead by Lucross. He pushed into the room and looked around.

"Clear," he said. The rest of them pushed in, searching the area.

The room wasn't very big, only the size of a small school classroom. There wasn't much to begin with, desks lined along the walls, and what was in there was covered in dust.

Across the empty space was a large, active cryo-pod. The glass in the window was frosted over, and the air was cold, mists flowing lightly through the room. Chris couldn't make out whoever was inside.

"Who is this?" Katherine asked, trying to peer into the frozen glass.

"There's a name on the pod," Lucross said, wiping the frost from the nametag. "Victoria. No last name, no information. Must've worked here and frozen herself when the incident occurred."

"Interesting," Chris said, staring blankly at the name. "Think we should wake her?"

"Not now," Lucross said. "We don't have time, or the extra space onboard the *SnapShot* to support another person." He paused and looked back at the pod. Chris could see that Lucross wanted to help. She probably had information regarding the planet, and whatever may have occurred there. "Let's get going."

They backed out of the room again, Chris taking one more look over to the pod. *Victoria.* He swore that one day he would return and find out who she was. *What an adventure that would be!* Until then, he needed to focus on the mission.

Chris moved out and caught up with the rest of his team, who were already planting the second charge on the yellow door. Katherine set the timer as before, and they moved back down the hall and waited. The blast was quick, and it echoed through the empty structure with ease. The door was breached, and they quickly pushed inside.

This room was bigger than that which Victoria was sleeping in. If Chris had to guess, the size of a basketball court, maybe larger.

To contrast such a spacious room, there wasn't anything inside, save a pedestal in the middle. On top of the glowing blue pedestal was a device the size of a small crate. It had hundreds of components, though there seemed to be only one button. As Chris moved closer, he could see the moniker "*Particle Breaker*" printed beneath the device.

"Is this it?" James asked, confused. "This is what we went through all this trouble for?"

"What the hell even is it?" Amabel asked. "It certainly looks odd, and it's a lot smaller than what I expected we'd find."

Lucross picked it up slowly, making sure not to damage it as he gently placed it into his bag.

"Alright," he said, hoisting the bag onto his shoulder, "let's get out of here. We've seen enough." They moved out fast. Just as they were going back into the stairwell, Chris caught sight of an elevator. The elevator to the core.

"You guys go on ahead," he said as he started making his way to the elevator. "I want to check something really quick."

"Brennan, no," Lucross yelled to him. "We don't have time for this."

"Just go on, I'll catch up."

"Well," Lucross sighed, "if you're leaving, you're not going alone. Frost, go with him. Make sure he doesn't do anything stupid. We'll go scout out the Hyperdrive and all rendezvous at the ship. Clear?"

"Yes sir," Katherine and Chris said in unison. The elevator doors opened and they scuttled inside, watching their team leave as the doors closed again.

The elevator began moving down, and it was moving fast. Chris felt his weight lift from him, as though he were light as a feather. They had 20 kilometers to travel, so he knew it would take a couple of minutes at the speed in which they were falling.

"Chris?" Katherine called to him softly, a hint of nervousness on her tongue. "Where exactly are we going?"

"To the core of the planet. This place was built for containment, and I want to figure out what it is they're keeping down here."

"Why does it matter?"

"Think about it," Chris began to explain, "this place is a scientific goldmine. A hollow planet, constructed by the Homage government around something they must have thought was dangerous. The gravity here can't be generated by machine, the surface area of the world is far too wide. They constructed hundreds of buildings, with hundreds of rooms for thousands of experiments. And all of them were kept secret from the rest of the galaxy. Why do you think this place was kept for so long?"

"I'd assume because it's dangerous. I mean, there was an accident here, remember?"

"Then why isn't there any sign of danger? No *signs* of anything dangerous? We have yet to encounter any real threats. There're no toxins in the air, no seismic activity. What's so scary about a planet made by man? Obviously it's structurally sound, considering it has survived so long. I want to find out its secrets."

"Okay, well, at least you're not doing it alone."

"We'll be okay. There can't be anything too dangerous, right?" He smiled at her, and she smiled back.

The elevator began to slow, adding weight back to Chris' body. He took one more look at Katherine before the elevator came to a halt. The doors began to slide open, and the small structure began to fill with a blinding bright light.

Chris instinctively shut his eyes tight. He reached to his belt and grabbed his glasses, throwing them onto his face and allowing them time to adjust to the light.

Chris opened his eyes, his lenses dark enough to contradict the shine penetrating the doorway. He looked over to Katherine, who had done the same. Carefully, he took a step outside and looked around. He was on a walkway hooked to the ceiling of the planet. The walkways stretched all the way around and across the metallic crust of Ljuska. From where he was, there wasn't much to see. Just a bright, empty, spherical chasm so large that he couldn't see the other side with any clarity.

"Well, where is it?" Katherine asked, looking around with him. There was a loud crackling beneath them, like electricity dashing around.

There's something beneath us. Chris put his hands on the railing and looked down from the walkway.

What the hell is that?

Underneath them, filling up the entirety of the core below, was a large, shining crack. It was floating there, in empty space, extending from one end of the planet to the other. It was just as the schematics of the planet had shown. It would flash every few seconds, cracking and emitting a long, high whooshing sound.

"Chris." Katherine was scared. She wasn't the only one. "What exactly am I looking at?"

"The biggest secret the Homage government has kept from us," he whispered back to her. He was so taken aback, so shocked. He couldn't think. *What the hell is it?*

He sat down and pulled his laptop out, quickly scrolling through the many documents he had downloaded from the manager's computer. Further and further into the documented secrets he went until one of them caught his eye. It was a fifty-page document, simply titled *"Rift"*. He whispered the word to himself over and over before finally opening the file.

The report was filed by the former Homage Lead Scientist and First Captain, who seemed to be the same person. Chris began reading aloud:

> *"The rift was opened on March 16, 2575 outside of the M2-9 Nebula, commonly known as the Cosmic Butterfly. The sheer size of the rift was no more than an incident, a fluke in the technology I had developed.*
>
> *The intent of my project was to create a small ripple in the fabric of reality, no more than the size of a pencil. However, the rift grew to be a million times the intended size, large enough for objects, animals, and even terrain to come through from different time periods throughout the history of the universe.*
>
> *This was all done with the device that my former partner and I had developed: The Particle Breaker. Using this device, we could accelerate the charges of multiple protons and electrons while keeping them in*

a contained environment. This containment forced them to find another means of escape, caused them to break through the fabric of reality and through the time stream.

Though there is no history of the rift being present in other time periods, prehistoric, early organisms and structures began to be pulled through, such as dinosaurs and plant matter. To stop those from dying and to help study my creation, I advised the Homage Council of Earth to begin construction of a sort of Shield World, to encase the rift and the danger it might have posed on the galaxy.

Now, after taking 125 years to observe and study it, I look to collect my observations.

The rift seems to have mass, as it produces its own earth-like gravity. This was helpful to us, as it relieved our construction team of having to install gravity generators across the surface of Ljuska. Long term scans discovered that it was made up of every known element in the universe, as well as those that were undiscovered. This was expected, as it is a portal throughout time and space. Naturally, we detect every element in all of time and space.

So far, we have not been able to find a way for our team to shut the rift if it becomes more unstable, or a way to pinpoint a destination if ever pulled in, but I have a feeling that we'll get that technology developed soon. Until then, I will continue to receive observational reports as I lead the Homage army in the war."

Chris shut his laptop, and looked up at Katherine, whose eyes were wide and staring blankly. He slowly turned his view from her back down to the rift.

"That's a rift in time?" Katherine asked, her voice shaking. She was almost as scared as he was, if not more.

"It's not possible," he replied, his voice almost inaudible. He couldn't tear his eyes away from the rift, no matter how much he willed himself to look away.

Now even through his glasses, it was blinding. He thought he could feel its power showering onto him. "There's no such thing as a rift in time. Time travel is impossible."

"I guess not."

He was still glaring into the rift, when there was a sudden sharp pain in his brain. It was as though his temporal lobes were pounding, trying to break free of his skull.

He collapsed onto the walkway, curling into fetal position and putting his hands on his head. Images of people and places began to flash before his eyes. He tried to swat them away, but his hand only met metal. What was this rift doing to him?

Voices were playing in the back of his mind, some crying, some screaming, and others laughing. He started to spasm, his body hitting the floor and railing repeatedly. He could hear Katherine calling to him, screaming his name over and over.

"I love you, Christopher," was the last thing he heard. It wasn't long before he blacked out.

7

19th September 2753 14:22:59

Katherines voice called to him. He could hear her, clear as day, but that's not what he was trying to focus on.

Chris had woken up in his bedroom again. This time, he knew it wasn't real. He was back in his dream. The same dream he was given during the battle of Texas.

His head didn't hurt this time. There weren't any memories or barriers trying to throw themselves back into place in his mind. There was no need to.

Because he remembered.

Peering into the rift allowed whatever barriers in his mind to free him. He was in control, but the flood of memories was too much for him to handle. The overflow had caused him to pass out, resulting in his first real visit to the dreamscape.

He threw the covers off himself and stood up, looking around at the room he had artfully crafted. There were no flaws in his design, and nothing was dirty.

How could it have been? He hadn't been there in fifty years.

Walking cautiously to the door, he opened it to see the red-eyed woman sitting at the dining room table again, reading an old magazine. She must've heard the door open, because she looked up to see him coming through. When she caught sight of him, her face filled with worry.

"Christopher," she said, standing up and moving swiftly toward him. He smiled as she approached, relieved to see that she was doing well. "Oh my God, are you okay? You seemed so wracked the last time you were here, and that was over a month ago!"

Chris reached out and grabbed hold of her hands, considering her burning eyes with a large grin on his face.

"Hello Victoria," he said as he embraced his sister in a tight hug. "Damn, do I have a story for you."

#

Chris began to wake up, following Katherines voice through the rest still calling him. He slowly opened his eyes and looked up at her.

"Oh my God, Chris!" She exclaimed, pulling him into a tight hug. "Are you okay? I was so worried about you. I tried shaking you and everything but you wouldn't wake up."

"I'm fine, Katherine," he said calmly. "Nothing to worry about. The complexity of our situation must have made me lightheaded. I fainted, that's all."

"Really?" she said, pulling away from him and looking in his eyes. "It seemed a lot worse than a blackout."

"I'm okay." He stood up and looked back down at the rift. Whatever had happened, he couldn't let her know. *Not yet.* "Let's regroup with the others. Have you tried communicating with them?"

"Well, yes, but," she paused, pointing at the ceiling, "lead frame."

"Right. Let's get going."

They walked into the elevator and Chris hit the button for them to ascend. The lift moved quickly, working to combat the gravitational pull of the rift. Katherine didn't say much on the way up, which mildly worried Chris. Normally she would jump at the chance of conversation.

A ding filled the elevator as it came to a halt. Chris stepped out and Katherine followed closely. He glanced towards the room where Victoria was sleeping, wondering when he would get the chance to talk to her again.

They made their way through Response once more, and climbed out using a rope left behind by Lucross and the others. Chris cringed once he reentered the sunlight.

"Hey," he said, lifting his comms device to his face. "What's the progress on retrieving the Hyperdrive?" He waited for a second until another voice cracked through.

"*We already found it,*" Samantha's voice said. "*We detached it, and Lucross took the bike back to the ship so that we don't have to make our journey again. Once he's there, he'll come pick us up.*"

"Roger that. See you guys soon."

Chris sat down on the soft grass surrounding the opening of Response, pulling his laptop out. He opened a lot of his old files and reports, intent on reading through all of them. His returning memories were pristine, but he wanted to recap everything that had happened on Ljuska before the parasitic incident, just to be sure.

"What are you reading?" Katherine asked, curious as to why he was staring so intensely at the screen.

"I'm looking at old reports that were filed and stored on the manager's computer," he told her, glancing up from time to time. "Trying to understand and establish a history of this shell-planet, or at least this specific research data. It's not really important, I'm just curious."

"Mind if I read along?"

"Not at all." She sat down behind him and began reading over his shoulder, looking through one classified document after another.

The subjects ranged over many different genres. Some were studies about the rift and its behavior, while others were biological studies about whatever might have come through it.

There were studies on dinosaurs and other ancient creatures, the different types of flora and fauna, some starships or parts, advanced tech, and many more. The rift was a goldmine of information throughout time and space, and Chris made sure to take advantage of this in the past.

He was the one who had written many of the reports, and he made sure never to put his name on any of them. It was a good thing, as it would be terribly complicated to explain to Katherine how he – a twenty-eight-year-old Special Forces soldier – had written and signed documents from fifty to one hundred years beforehand.

It was better none of them knew the truth. *Not yet.*

The two didn't have to wait long before Lucross brought the *SnapShot* and the rest of the team to Response. From one look, Chris could see that the damages had been repaired and the ship was fully functional.

Once the two were safely onboard, they met up with the rest of the team.

"Alright," Lucross began, now that everyone was present around him, "mission accomplished. We were able to retrieve what we were sent for. Now, there's just one more problem before we head home."

"What?" Amabel said, puzzled.

"That." Lucross pointed out of the main window towards the skyline beyond, and it took everyone a second to understand what he meant. "The shield. We can't knock it out by force from the inside, so we're going to need to find a way to turn the damn thing off from the ground."

"How are we going to do that?"

"Chris, you have a map, right?" He said, turning his attention towards Chris and his laptop. "Think you could find the shield generator?"

"There are multiple generators, each covering a different section of the planet," Chris said, pulling the map up on his screen and projecting it to the main monitor in the ship.

"So how do we take it down?"

"We don't. Not the whole thing." Chris walked up to the screen and pointed to the nearest generator site, just a few kilometers from their position. "If we take just one of them down temporarily, a section of the shield will dissipate, and we'll be able to make our escape with time to spare."

"Alright, that sounds like a pretty decent plan."

"How d'you know all of this?" James asked, looking at Chris mysteriously. "You make it sound like you've been here before."

"If I had been here before, we'd already be on our way home," Chris snapped back. "You guys took your sweet time getting to us, so I decided to do some research while we waited."

"It's true," Katherine piped in, "he did. I read it with him."

"What the hell has gotten into you two?" Samantha demanded, looking angrily at James and Chris. "There's no way that Chris could have ever been here before, James. He's not even a quarter of our ages."

"Alright, enough!" Lucross yelled at them, causing them all to snap shut. "We need to get this done, now. The more time we waste, the less likely we are to win this damn war. Brennan: punch the coordinates into the computer and set it to autopilot. Everyone else is dismissed until we get there. Understood?"

"Yes sir," everyone piped. Chris did as he was told and went straight into his room, ignoring everyone else.

He was honestly glad that James had snapped. He needed some alone time anyway. Something in his mind felt fuzzy.

Now that Chris had his memories back, he wasn't sure what he should do. He knew it would be best for him to keep it a secret from the rest of his team.

Once they got back to Earth, he was going to have a word with Alterous. Alterous was the only person that knew who Chris really was, which explained the look he received during the assignment and the use of his full name.

Chris created a new document on his laptop and began typing:

September 19th, 2753

It has been over fifty years since I have made a new entry under this name. It has taken me a lot longer than expected, but I finally have my memories back.

I remember everything. Caroline, the rift, the experiments.

My mission.

I know I am not too late to live up to the expectations bestowed upon me, and I intend to see this through to the end. I owe it to all the people I have had to watch die. My parents, lovers, shipmates and crews, friends. All the people that I miss more than anything else in the universe. This is for them.

In the time that I've been gone, the war has progressively worsened. The Homage front is almost destroyed, and there seems to be no hope left for the galaxy. Whatever the Council thinks they're going to do with the Particle Breaker better work, or else I've got a lot more work to do.

I didn't spend 900 years just to fail.
-Christopher Brennan

He shut his laptop and set it next to him. There wasn't much else he could do until he reached the end of his journey.

"*Shield generator coming up,*" Lucross said over comms. "*Brennan, get out and do your thing.*" Chris could feel the *SnapShot* touch down onto the artificial ground. He stood up and made his way out of the ship, not bothering to talk to anyone.

Jogging out, Chris caught sight of the familiar shield generator that he had set up before his departure. It was a small, rectangular, full metal building with a sharp spire on top. The spire extended into a thin particle beam that connected to the shield above them, producing the thick red shell encasing the smaller Shield World.

He made his way inside and moved to the control panel on the central mechanism. He straightaway typed in the passcode and set a timer of five minutes for the generator to stall.

It would give them enough time to escape before it reasserted itself. Before leaving, he grabbed the generator's remote deactivation control and muscled it into one of the many pouches on his belt.

"Five minutes," he said as he entered back into the ship. Again, he didn't stop to talk, and didn't even bother to make eye contact. He just took a straight path to his bedroom.

"Alright people, hold on," James said before Chris' door had finished sliding shut behind him. Chris sat on his bed as he felt the ship swing and rocket into the atmosphere. He liked the feeling of the different forces pressing against him. It reminded him of home.

A minute later, the forces ceased and they were out into the void again.

"We're going t'use the Hyperdrive's full potential this time," James said over comms. *"Now that we know it works. We'll be back t'Sol in about twenty-six days."*

Chris sank into his mattress, relaxing as the drive kicked into gear and took them into the dark. A shorter trip was fine, if he was given time to get himself together.

Christopher Brennan was back. And this time, he was here to stay.

8

July 28th, 2566

Finally got the approval from the Council of Earth to conduct my experiment.

I have worked twenty long, exhausting years to finally come to this moment. There is, however, one drawback: my partner is dead.

Just fifteen hours ago, my partner and close friend Jackson Augustine passed away in the Margin Military Hospital on Pan. Incidents and genetic mutations can still occur in human beings, despite their wonder drug that prolongs the duration of the body. And, even now, there still is no real cure for cancer. New treatments and developments have come up, of course, using biological matter from countless other planets and cultures. And most of the time, they worked.

Jack was just too far gone by the time treatments began. It was too late.

So, this I do in his name. He poured what was left of his short life into this research, and I intend to make the most of the results. From now on, he will be added to the list of reasons as to why I will complete my mission. This is for HIM. For THEM.

For EVERYONE.

Of course, all the tech is experimental. Nobody has ever opened a rift in time before, not even God. I will write more once preparations are being made.

-First Captain Christopher Brennan

\#

January 5th, 2568

Preparations almost complete. The Council is providing me with everything I need to make sure this all works out. I swore that the Particle Breaker will work, though I'm nowhere near certain about anything. It's all theoretical.

They have chosen to provide me with a new Behemoth-*class space vessel (against my good wishes), and a stationed research facility to observe the rift once it opens (IF it opens). These two things have impeded progress, and added another three years onto our wait time.*

In the meantime, I must choose a location in which to test the Particle Breaker. It needs to be somewhere isolated from the rest of explored space, from all three divisions. The Milky Way is HUGE, so there are still plenty of unexplored territories to pick from.

Until then, I remain fighting on the fronts of the war, all over the damn void. We've lost nine colonies in just the past seven days. There was nothing I could do to save them, but I can do everything in my limited power to avenge all that they stood for.

-First Captain Christopher Brennan
#
April 12th, 2571

Construction of the two structures provided by the Council have finished production, and are now being moved to the launch stations, where I am also headed.

Per design and research, the station should be able to travel in Hyperspace, even though there is no guarantee. Though I wouldn't mind losing it (as I did not want it in the first place), I do not intend to let the Homage's scarce resources go to waste. Not because of me.

I have chosen a destination to which we will be traveling. That, of course, is the nearby Twin-Jet Nebula, M2-9. It was always my favorite space-faring superstructure, and its more common name – The Cosmic Butterfly – astounds me. I have found that this would be the best place to conduct my experiment. It's isolated, unexplored, and mostly uninhabitable. We won't be bothered there. Not for a very long time.

Unfortunately, the system is 2100 light-years away. So, even at our top speeds, it may take us another three years just to reach it. This will provide ample time to prepare the research facility and such, while I make adjustments to the Particle Breaker.

I cannot believe that this is happening, even as I witness the construction of vessels designed just for me, and to my specifications. I have never been so excited in my life. This isn't necessary to my mission. Nobody has asked me to do this. This is done because I want to do it.

I have my own free will for once. I hope He doesn't get mad.

-First Captain Christopher Brennan

#

February 7th, 2573

Still in Hyperspace, traveling at faster-than-light speeds.

It has been an extremely long time, but I've been making the most of it. I spend my time moving around the facility, making sure everything stays intact. I have also made some adjustments to my machine, hopefully allowing for more accurate results.

I barely sleep. But when I do, at least I'm accompanied. Victoria is the most important person in my life, and she's the only one who hasn't gone on without me. With her consent, I froze her long ago in Cryo. She sleeps, and sleeps. It saddens me that she stays that way, but she gladly chose it in order to maintain our relationship. She's my sister, and I'm not sure what I'd do without her in my life.

She lives in a dream world that I was able to craft for her, though she lives alone. When she's there, she experiences everything in real time, unlike when she chooses to sleep. Her body is back on Earth, in the main hospital facility on Easter Island.

I miss her. The last time I had actually woke her up was fifteen years ago.

We will be exiting Hyperspace in about another year, so I will continue to make adjustments. My excitement grows. Even He must be curious to see what will happen.

-First Captain Christopher Brennan

#

March 17th, 2575

I made a huge mistake. And I mean that VERY literally.

The rift is open, and the experiment worked. There's just one very large problem. I miscalculated.

The rift was only supposed to be the length of a pencil. Small, easily accessible and maintained. But I guess the Particle Breaker must have malfunctioned, or I had made the wrong adjustments at some time between then and now.

The rift currently measures at 25,000 km from end to end. That's nearly twice the diameter of the Earth. It also seems to have some sort of gravitational pull. When it ripped open, my ship – Infinite Tide – was almost sucked in by the unexpected force, and a couple of the smaller ships were lost.

I'm not entirely sure what I should do. I'll relay a message to Alterous and the rest of the Council, but until they respond...

I'll make observations. There's nothing else I CAN do. I won't use my high level of influence yet. Not for this. It poses no immediate danger.

-First Captain Christopher Brennan
#
April 27th, 2583

Ljuska is under construction now. I sit here in my quarters on the Infinite Tide, *watching through the window as materials shipped from all over the colonies are welded and torn together to form a shell around the Rift.*

I have now been named Chief Scientist of the Homage Government, as well as First Captain. My job is to research the Rift, and as such, conduct further experiments AND lead the Homage military through the war.

Materials have started coming through the Rift, such as rock, dirt and water. We've decided to gather these things and spread them across the surface of Ljuska, making it a planet-like structure. Unless they went to the core, nobody would be able to tell the world was artificial. Many facilities are being built beforehand, the structures showing until they get buried in the new materials.

I'm not too sure what we'll learn, or what else will come through, but I'm hopeful. For now, we're not going to send anything through until we can gain some sort of control.

-Chief Scientist, First Captain Christopher Brennan

#

Chris closed his laptop and yanked out the USB drive. He stared at the very thing he had risked his past life and memory for, shuddering as the feelings of the cold void ran through him again.

"Exiting Hyperspace now," James' voice broadcasted through comms. *"Welcome back to Sol."*

Chris looked out of his window, watching as the blackness outside died down, the many objects of the terrestrial plane coming into view. As they proceeded, so did the terrifying reality.

"Mayday, mayday!" a voice shot through the comms. *"This is the captain of the UEA Classic Drive requesting assistance. Multiple Terran vessels have just exited*

Hyperspace, and are headed straight for Earth. We've been hit, status: critical."

Looking through the window, Chris watched as hundreds of ships came into view, many of them damaged. Fighters flew throughout the space between ships, firing projectiles and lasers at one another without care for anyone or anything around them.

The *SnapShot* was just passing Mars, whose thin atmosphere seemed to be filled with the flaming wreckage of the many damned vessels.

He caught view of the *Classic Drive* just before it burst to pieces, the screams of the crew coming in through the static before it cut out.

"Aren't we going to do anything to help them?" Chris yelled angrily as he ran into the main deck.

"We have a mission to complete," Lucross answered coldly, standing behind James and staring out the front of the ship. "Once that is done, we will receive orders on what we do."

James didn't say a word, and didn't even bother to turn around. Chris could tell that James was uncomfortable.

"Those people need our help, and we are perfectly capable!"

"That is not for you to decide."

Chris felt his fist clench tight, and he couldn't believe he was actually thinking about fighting his superior.

"Chris…" Katherine said behind him, putting her hand on his shoulder. He yanked himself away, staring intensely at Lucross, whose back was still facing him.

"How much longer until we reach Earth?" he muttered.

"About thirteen minutes," James said, still refusing to turn around.

Chris turned and stormed back to his room. He knew that it wasn't their task to help the other ships in the fleet, but they had every reason to disobey orders. People needed their help, and now they were dying. He'd make sure their deaths weren't in vain.

9
16th October 2753 11:42:37

"Report, and make it quick," Alterous barked at the team as they entered the Council chamber.

The room was chaotic, and Council members were scrambling over news of the recent Terran attacks. Many had screens up and mics on, pushing orders through to the fleet and viewing the fights through many interplanetary cameras.

Chris could catch glimpses of the brutal scenes, ships and people being ripped to shreds in the unwavering vacuum of space. Each one made him cringe, and only fueled his rage.

"Sir," Lucross began. "After successfully using the provided Hyperdrive and traveling to Ljuska, we were able to penetrate the shield and trek across the surface. We reached the facility the device was stored in, and retrieved it as instructed."

"Good, good," Alterous said, looking up at them with brighter eyes. "Where is the device now?"

"In the hold of our ship, sir."

"Understood, I will send a team to retrieve it right away. I assume that you figured out what the device is?"

"No, sir."

"Actually," Chris spoke up, looking Alterous in the eyes, "I read some old documents, along with Katherine, and we were able to figure out what the device does."

He grinned slyly up at Alterous, who read the message clearly.

"Is that so?" He returned Chris' smile. "Well, I had best inform the rest of the team, then." Lucross glared over at Chris and Katherine mistrustfully. "What you six went so far to retrieve is called the Particle Breaker. This machine, built by one of the greatest minds in human history, has the power to open a rift in time."

The rest of his team taken was aback by the latest information, and this only amused Chris.

"Why would we need such a device?" Amabel asked. "I don't see how time travel will help us now."

"We need it because we are going to open a new rift. But this time, it will be controlled and forced down to the size of a starship." He paused, and the rest of the Council members ceased their individual tasks to listen to what he had to say.

"We debated this matter for months," a member with the last name Jackson informed them. "Even during the time that you all were gone, and *we* were left to defend the Earth. The moral implications are complicated, but we've all come to agree that this is the best – and really, the only – course of action left to take."

"Even so," Alterous continued, "there is not a choice anymore. We need to finish this war topside. We will not explain the rest of the plan until we are certain of the date we wish to proceed. There is a bigger task we need to complete in order for this to work."

"Until then, you all will remain here, at the Council base. As you wait, your ship will be upgraded and repaired as need be."

"Dismissed."

The team began to walk away as the Council went back to their heavy business, towards the door they had been quickly pulled through.

Everyone except for Chris. He stood at attention, stiff as an iron rod, waiting. Once the team realized, they quickly turned around and tried to quietly usher him out.

He ignored their calls, however, and continued to stand still. Alterous looked down at him with a raised eyebrow.

"Is there something I can help you with, Brennan?"

"Sir," Chris started, "may I have a word with you? In private?" His team gasped and mumbled beneath their breath, but he ignored them and maintained his eye contact with the Council Leader.

"Sure thing, Christopher. Give me just a moment." Alterous looked to the rest of the team again. "I believe I dismissed the rest of you," he barked at them, his role as Leader protruding. "Brennan, go stand over there," he pointed to the left side of the Council chamber, to a spot that wouldn't be visible to anyone but security. "I will be there in a second."

"Yes sir." Chris strode over to the designated spot and waited patiently. Soon enough, Alterous stepped down and over to Chris. They looked one another in the eyes for a second before embracing in a hug and laughing quietly.

"It sure took you long enough," Alterous chuckled. "Twenty years, you told us. You did not even wake up for an extra thirty."

"I guess I miscalculated," Chris said, breaking from the embrace of his old friend. "We both know it's not the first time. What did I miss?"

"Well, obviously, the war is raging on. We have lost plenty more colonies in the past fifty years, but now they're being ignored. The Terran forces have decided to focus one hundred percent of their power on the Earth. Cultural origin or not, I think they just mean to destroy the planet."

"Damn. A lot worse than I had predicted. I shouldn't have slept for so long, I could've helped more."

"That is one of many reasons we sent your team to Ljuska. Christopher, you have done more than any other man during this time. Do not sell yourself out. Though, a little bit of your power may come in handy at a time like this."

"I can't," Chris said, shaking his head. "Not now, anyway. Having my memories blocked for so long has dampened my abilities. Besides, I look to keep my identity a secret until after we win. The last thing we need is my team being wracked by my true nature during the final conflict."

"You really think we will win?"

"I know your plan," Chris said with a smile. "Figured it out almost as soon as I returned. And I think full-well that it will work."

"As sharp as ever, I see."

"Who do you intend to send through?"

"Not your team, if that is what you're asking. We will be sending the best, most powerful ships we have, but there is no guarantee that they will make it back. And I do not want to leave it up to chance with your team."

"I see. I'm sure it will all go smoothly, then."

"It is great to have you back, Christopher." Alterous sighed, letting go of all the stress he'd been maintaining for a brief second. "I have been in need of your insight for a long time. I do not know how we were able to hold up while you have been away."

"You have been doing an excellent job. Better than what was ever asked of you. You just need to pull through for a bit longer. I'm back, and I'll be here whenever you need me."

"Alright," Alterous straightened himself up again, "I better get back to work. There is a lot going on, as I am sure you've noticed."

He hugged Chris one more time before swiftly making his way back up to the stands, where calls and reports surely awaited him. Chris left the chamber, proceeding to wherever his team had been escorted.

#

The team had been led to some sort of extra dormitory, installed for visitors. Fully furnished and built up with the latest technology and luxuries. It was a place for kings, not soldiers.

Chris was surprised, but not so much as when he saw the looks on his friends faces. Each one was filled to the brim with suspicion and worry.

"What did you need to talk to Alterous about?" Lucross demanded as Chris moved in.

"Personal matters," Chris replied coldly, striding passed him. Stopping, he turned back and looked Lucross in the eyes. Chris knew exactly what Lucross would say next. "Which translates to 'none of your business', so don't bother asking any further." With this, he made his way back to the room he assumed was his own.

Other than his unwillingness to help the ships in need, Chris was becoming frustrated with how different Lucross seemed to be acting. More authoritative and suspicious, as if they hadn't been friends for years. Granted, Chris was different, but Lucross didn't know that.

Chris laid on his new bed, thinking about the day's events as he so commonly does, a buzz still itching deep in his mind. Things had been getting complicated, especially with the late, unforeseen reemergence of his memories.

He was just glad that he was able to reconnect with Alterous after so many years. Chris knew that it was rare to find people who remembered him, let alone those he had become friends with. His identity was to be kept secret from the rest of the Homage division and military personnel until it returned to him.

Those were the protocols he had set up before the incident outside of the Khal system.

All he needed to do was figure out how to keep his identity hidden until the end of the war. He'd been acting different, there was no hiding that. He'd done too much in front of the team for him to ease their suspicions. A hole was being dug, but as long as he lasted until the Cessation, he'd be able to crawl out before it got too deep.

There was a knock on the door and Amabel let herself in.

"Brennen," she started before he had time to react, "I don't know what's going on with you, or with everyone else. We don't need to be fighting one another at a time like this." She was furious, and he could tell that she meant it. "We're friends. You are one of my best friends! If we don't stick together now, we're going to fall apart and we're going to lose this war."

"I see..." he said, stopping himself short. "I understand. I'm sorry, I don't know what's been getting into me. It's been a long day and I need some rest." He didn't know what else to tell her. There wasn't anything he could really say to make her feel better.

There was something different about Lucross, and Chris could tell it was on Amabel's mind as well. He could see it in her eyes. "I'll be better," he assured her. "I promise."

"Okay...thank you for listening to me. Trust me, it's a long, odd time for me as well."

"I understand," he said, putting a hand on her shoulder. "Be careful, okay?"

"I will." With that, she left the room. Chris laid back again, pondering what had influenced her to talk with him. She was never usually like that. Something was bothering her.

Chris closed his eyes, deciding to nap until their next assignment.

<u>10</u>
16th October 2753 22:19:50

"That's one hell of a story, Christopher," Victoria said, setting down the ceramic mug she had been drinking from. "Why do you think it took so long?"

"Honestly? I have no idea." He shook his head and pinched between his eyes. "I should have woken up thirty years ago. Feel like it must've been some sort of divine intervention."

"I doubt the Creator would meddle in such things, don't you think?"

"I'm not sure what else could have happened. It was either him, or my life has finally been taking its toll. I mean, nine hundred years? There's no organism in the universe who could hope to live as long as I have."

"I guess it's all up in smoke for now."

"Yeah," Chris said, lazily looking around the room. His focus pulled into a picture on the far wall, by the stove of the kitchen. Two parents, both happy and with their equally ecstatic children. "Do you think mom and dad would be proud of me? Of everything I've done?" His eyes drifted back to her, their sky-blue color full of sincerity.

"More than you could dream of," Victoria replied, grabbing hold of one of Chris' hands. "You were always the favorite, you know."

"That's just because I'm 'special'. Because of who I was born to be. They weren't around long enough to see who I would become. What my actions would cause, and what I'd lead others to do. I've taken almost as many lives as I have sworn to save. This whole bloody war is my fault! I was never given enough instruction to what I should do during my life, and it's led to such a big catastrophe! And now. Now they plan on using another one of my inventions as a weapon."

"What do you mean?" she asked, holding her mug in front of her face so she could see just above the lip.

"The Particle Breaker." He sighed. "Before my memories came back, the Council sent me and my team to retrieve it from Ljuska. They plan on opening another, more condensed rift."

"Christopher, that isn't good. That invention wasn't meant for interplanetary war, but for observation and study."

"I know, Victoria. I'm the one who built it."

She sat her mug down and stood up, walking behind Chris and putting her hands on his shoulders. Chris could almost hear her think, the fire in her eyes brightening again and again.

"Do you think it will work?" she pondered to him.

"I have my hopes. Either way, once this war has ended, I'm coming back to Ljuska. I'm going to wake you up."

"Wait, really?" Chris could hear the concealed excitement in her voice as her eyes brightened significantly.

"Yes. Once there, we'll live on. Away from the turmoil sprung up in these damned divisions. We could build a colony there, perhaps."

"That sounds amazing, brother."

Chris heard a knock on his door, off where the real world crossed into his dream. New orders. "I have to go," Chris said, standing and turning to look her in the eyes. They dimmed with disappointment. She didn't want him to leave again. "I promise I'll be back soon, okay?"

"Okay." She pulled him into a hug, clinging to him with desperation. When they broke, she looked up to see that he had disappeared.

Chris felt his consciousness fall back into the physical world, his eyes fluttering open as he became fully aware.

The knocking continued, which was odd. If it were something important, they would have just let themselves in. The knocking just went on and on, constantly changing tones.

"Come in," Chris called out to his visitor, not bothering to waste energy sitting up. He looked towards the door and watched as James led himself into the room.

"Hey," James muttered, shutting the door behind him and sitting in a chair towards the end of Chris' bed. "How you feelin'?"

"I'm just fine, thank you."

"Good, good." His voice trailed off, and his mind went to a different place for only a second when he snapped back. "Hey man, look. I'm sorry about the way I acted at Ljuska. And for not botherin' t'talk to you at any point afterwards. It wasn't cool of me t'be so assaultin' the way I was, and you didn't deserve it." Chris smiled as he heard this.

"Hey, don't worry about it. I was in a bad place, too. I shouldn't have been so defensive."

"You're my best friend, man. Even though I may not act like it sometimes, I do care about you. And you've been actin' pretty strange as of late. What's been goin' on?"

Chris didn't know what to say. This whole time, he had been blowing it all away, telling the team that he was fine. That he was just sick. It would help if he could tell James the truth.

"My memories," Chris blurted out, deciding it would be best to tell someone what was really going on. "My amnesia is fading and my memories are finally returning." *At least, a part of the truth.*

"Are you serious!? Why didn't you say anythin' about it before?"

"Because at first I wasn't sure. But after remembering Tyler, things kept coming to me. Now, they're back completely."

"Well c'mon, tell me! Who were you before becomin' the modern Chris Brennan we've come t'know and love?"

"I'd rather not talk about it right now," Chris chuckled, playing it off. In fact, he wasn't sure of the answer himself.

"We should tell the rest of our team," James stood, making his way to the door again.

"No no no," Chris stood and grabbed him before he could leave the room. "I don't think that's such a promising idea. With everything that's been going on, I think it would be best to keep the news out of earshot from anyone else. I don't want everyone getting overwhelmed and distracted from these important times."

"I see. Well, promise me that you'll tell us all about yerself once this war is over."

"Consider it done, man."

James smiled at Chris and left the room, leaving Chris alone with his thoughts. He sat and considered going back to sleep and spending time with Victoria, but that might prove to be difficult. He was wide awake now, and he had no idea when someone would wake him again.

"*Guys,*" Lucross' stiff voice came in through comms. "*We have a new assignment. We are to go throughout Sol and assist in whatever firefights we can until the Council gets what they need. Everyone to the* SnapShot, *now.*"

11
5th November 2753 07:17:32

The days were long. Every hour of each of the twenty days spent fighting in the void of the Sol system. Every minute used up, wondering how they would ever expect to hold their defensive line any longer.

Skirmish after skirmish, death after death, with both sides winning and losing with no real end in sight. UEASF fireteam Alpha wasn't sure about anything anymore. Everyone, except for Christopher Brennan.

Chris had been fighting alongside his team, pushing through almost one enemy starship a day, making sure to save as many lives as possible.

When they boarded enemy craft, he would take as many people as would admit surrender. They would become prisoners of war, but at least their lives would be spared. That was his goal.

His team, on the other hand, were more closed minded. They seemed to care about each successive objective, without bothering to care for loss of enemy life. He couldn't blame them, however. They were just doing their job, and wanted to end the war. Chris did, too. But he'd prefer to save more lives than he took.

Chris was in his room, throwing his combat suit back on after a quick two hours of sleep. He felt fully rested, but he knew that even his body would get exhausted before long. Once he had slipped on his suit and zipped it up, he stood and walked swiftly out onto the deck of the *SnapShot*. He moved over behind James, who was in the pilot seat, flying them towards their next target. Chris looked out to see the slender, *Behemoth*-class spacecraft hovering over the atmosphere of Mars.

Supposedly, this vessel was scanning the surface of Earth, scouting for weak points, and the location of the Council base. Alterous had contacted Chris about it, asking him to take care of the situation quickly.

Lucross and Amabel came up with their plan of action once Chris had informed them of the situation.

They were going to destroy the ships thrusters and attempt to ground it on the red surface of Mars. On the ground, they would infiltrate the vessel and destroy its systems, along with any information they may have had on the Earth's surface.

If they were correct, this craft would be outfitted for surveillance and research, not for combat.

Samantha and Katherine were stationed on the weapons systems, while Chris, Lucross and Amabel were to be the boarding crew. Chris grabbed a B-54 Burst Rifle and slung it onto his back, preparing himself for another day's work. Lucross was wielding an A-22, while Amabel held loosely onto her favorite pistol. Each one of them was fully prepared for their personal assault, and just needed to wait for the enemy to be grounded.

"Everyone ready?" James called out to the rest of the crew. One by one, they each pressed a button on their wrist comms. On a screen in front of James, green lights flashed for each of the members. "Alright, let's get on it. Light is green."

Chris felt the ship pivot and blast towards the enemy. The *SnapShot* swung around to the end of the ship and slowed towards the main thrusters. The *Behemoth* began to react to their movement, increasing its thrust and trying to move away from the nimbler attack craft.

"Knight, Frost!" Lucross called to Samantha and Katherine, respectively. "Open fire! Take down the damn ship."

"Aye," the two said as they began firing at the enemy. Chris and the others watched as blasts from their ship veered into the opposing vessel's thrusters, causing small and precise explosions all along their rims. The blue thrust began to fade, and the ship began to fall by the gravity of the Roman war planet. A complete success, as was usual.

They observed as the *Behemoth* fell into the thin atmosphere of the red planet, pieces of scrap metal burning and breaking off during the descent. It wasn't long before the ship made landfall.

"Alright, move out, Knight. We don't have time to waste."

"Yessir," James said, tilting the ship towards the crash site and accelerating. It was a minute before they came upon the enemy vessel. From what Chris could see, there must have only been one or two breaches in the hull. He wasn't sure how many people could have survived such a fall.

"Get us as close to the main server room as possible, and we'll take it from there. Amabel, Brennan, let's head to the door." Lucross tossed Chris and Amabel their respective helmets, and they pushed them on with ease. The helmets were to help their user to breath outside of hospitable environments, while their combat suits would keep them safe from the cold of the thin blanket of Carbon dioxide.

They walked to the main bay door and waited as James swung the ship starboard. The door began to groan open, and through it, they could see the quick-frozen hull of the *Behemoth*. They were positioned just above one of the breaches in the hull, nearest to the control center. Weapons in hand, they hopped out of the *SnapShot* and into the Terran abyss waiting beyond.

When they landed inside, Lucross brought up a holographic schematic of the typical *Behemoth*-class starship, with a point highlighted to show their intended destination. They were just two corridors away, so the trip would be short.

Chris looked around the hallway of the downed ship. Bodies of its crew had been thrown about, and most he could see were already freezing from the Martian air. He looked away again, shaking his head and focusing on the mission.

It's already too late. Boxes and other object were all strewn across the floors.

"*Move*," Lucross mumbled as they began to press forward. As they turned the first corner, a Terran came running out of one of the adjacent rooms, wielding a weapon. He fired towards the trio of his foes, though most of his shots riddled everywhere other than his targets. Chris moved behind a box to his left, while Lucross and Amabel dodged into a room to their right. As they tried to peek out the door, the Terran fired more projectiles their way, causing them to snap back.

Chris motioned to them with his hand in a circular motion, telling them to do it again. As they did, Chris looked over his cover, aimed down his sight and quickly fired a burst of rounds into his enemy's chest while he was distracted.

The Terrans body flopped down, limp and lifeless as the atmosphere wheezed from his suit. Amabel and Lucross moved back into the hallway as Chris stood up. Lucross gave the sign to continue, and they all began walking forward again. No other opposition stood in their way to the server control room, presumably all of them having been killed in the crash.

They approached the door to their target, which they found to be locked from the other side. Chris moved up, pulling an explosive charge from his belt and linking it up to the door.

They jumped back as the explosive detonated, blasting the doorway open and letting whatever air was in the room flow out into the hallway.

But with the abundance of oxygen, also came a large amount of gunfire. Lucross and Chris moved to the left of the doorway, and Amabel to the right. They waited until the shots finished out. Amabel unhooked a grenade from her belt and tossed it in, bracing herself.

They could hear yelling just before it detonated, blowing out a ton of debris. The three peered in, and saw Terran combatants strewn all over the room, blood and flesh scattered from one console to the next.

Stepping in, they moved around the room, placing charges on each of the machines and consoles. They had enough explosives to take out the entire ship but decided to focus on that room alone. It was their only objective, and they didn't want to overdo it.

They had almost finished placing the charges when a Bio-warrior jumped out from one of the large servers and tackled Chris to the ground. The sudden adversary grabbed hold of the detonator and crushed it between his large, modified hands.

Shocked, Chris punched the Bio square in the jaw, causing him to flail to the side in pain. Chris mounted his foe, proceeding to punch the Terran again and again in the head until he lay unconscious on the ground.

Breathing heavily and standing back up, Chris looked down at the crushed detonator with remorse, blood dripping from his gloved fist.

"*Well dandy,*" Amabel snarled over their helmet comms. "*Now what?*"

"Easy," Chris said, placing the final charge. "Let's get out of here."

Amabel led as Chris and Lucross followed her out. When they made it halfway down the corridor, he stopped, not saying a word to his mates as they carried on unaware of his absence.

Chris aimed down with his B-54, focusing his sights on one of the many charges strewn about the distant room. Just before he pulled the trigger, an announcement rang out through the *Behemoths* internal comms system.

"*This is a fleetwide alert from the president of Terra,*" the voice of a man called out. "*All Terran warships are to move beyond the Oort Cloud immediately. Do not delay. I repeat, do not delay.*"

Just after the message ended, another came through Chris' helmet.

"*Alpha team,*" Alterous' voice rang through. "*Return to Earth immediately, to the Council chambers. You are being reassigned.*" Chris smiled as Alterous cut back out. *You sly dog. How did you do it?*

Chris aimed back down and stared straight at the small bomb he had placed. He waited a second, then he pulled the trigger.

Boom. Before he knew it, he was thrown by the large blast through a window to the outside of the ship. He didn't bother trying to stand back up, his ears ringing as his whole body felt like it had been rocked hard. His combat suit was steaming from the heat it had absorbed from the explosion, dispersing it into the frigid air surrounding him. Looking towards the *Behemoth*, he watched as debris and singed shards of metal fell to the ground around him.

It was a terrifying sight, to be sure. A large, red-rimmed hole had been blown wide in the hull of the ship. Debris was strewn everywhere across the red, dusty terrain, and any fires that started were quickly blotted out by the freezing lack of oxygen. Among the debris, the bodies of the numerous soldiers and crew members were tossed around, many dismembered from the force of the blast, their flesh growing a new layer of frost.

Chris had been lucky.

"*Chris,*" Katherine called through the comms. "*Are you alright?*" He jerked his head to the right and watched as the *SnapShot* rocketed into view. It turned about and lowered itself until it landed ten meters away.

Chris slowly stood, his joints and muscles straining against the pain forced upon him by the explosion. He carefully checked his suit for any breaches, just to be sure, wincing as the pain spread through him like wildfire. Believing he was safe, he pivoted towards the *SnapShot* and hobbled his way to the opening bay doors. Stumbling in, he stopped and listened as the door closed once more.

Allowing the room a minute to pressurize, he tore away his helmet and took a deep breath as he threw it away from him. He took a few more rhythmic breathes before he tried to stand again.

He crumbled through the doorway and onto the deck, where he was greeted by his friends.

"You look like a mess," Samantha said, grabbing hold of one of his arms and leading him to his seat.

"Thanks," he chuckled back hoarsely. "I definitely feel like it."

"That was a very stupid thing to do," Lucross said, standing directly in front of Chris, his black and white hair hanging in front of his eyes as they pierced Chris.

"It was the only thing to do," Chris sniped back.

"Well. Respectable job." With that, Lucross walked away towards his quarters, his elegance seeming to have wavered over time.

"I'm just glad you're not too hurt," Katherine said, resting a hand on Chris' shoulder. This moment of contact sent a shivering wave down his spine. It was a feeling he couldn't describe, but he didn't like it.

"Yes," Chris said, "Well, I better rest while we're on our way to Earth." He stood up and staggered over to his room, pressing through the doorway and collapsing onto the bed. The *SnapShot* began to take off as he drifted into a deep sleep.

Back in the dream realm, Chris got up out of his bed and went to check on Victoria. He hadn't been sleeping much, so he knew she must've been lonely. Most people would be.

He strode into the kitchen, but he didn't see her there. It was her favorite place to sit and spend her time, so Chris thought it odd that she wasn't there.

"Victoria," Chris called out. He waited, but there was no response. His heartrate increased as he began to expect the worst. He scrambled through the rest of the house, throwing open doors and tossing aside furniture, calling her name again and again. *Where could she have gone?* Even if she had decided to sleep, his calls should've drawn her back into the dream.

Chris walked back out into the main room and stopped dead in his tracks. There, sitting on the couch that Chris had tossed aside, was a man. The man was slender and wore a very sleek suit. He had burning blue eyes, and a cunning smile that Chris could identify from a mile away.

"Hello brother," the stranger said, looking Chris dead in the eyes. "Hope you don't mind my visit, but I have a message from Father." His voice was gracefully British, tacked on the end with charm and swagger.

"What the hell are you doing here?" Chris moaned. He hated unwanted guests.

#

"We're comin' up t'the base now," James announced to everyone as he began their descent.

Chris had just woken up, rattled by the unexpected visit he had received. He was glad to make sure it would never happen again while he was alive.

The *SnapShot* was just entering the Council base when the team received another message from Alterous in text, rather than audio. In this message were detailed instructions for them to fly their ship through a series of tunnels inside of the base to reach another ship bay.

"Well damn," James said, looking over the instructions. "This'll be fun, I guess."

Chris watched over James' shoulder as he carefully willed the ship through the uncomfortably narrow tunnels. Although the *SnapShot* was long, it wasn't necessarily thin. The tips of the wings scratched the rocky surface of the passageways. Chris noticed that James winced with each impact. *He must really love this ship.*

The narrows were long, at least three kilometers in distance, with the diameter changing randomly again and again. It had taken them quite a few minutes, but eventually, they reached the end. And they were blown away.

At the end of the narrows was a larger ship bay, maybe twenty times bigger than the one they had just left. Unlike the other one, this bay was filled to the brim with all distinct kinds of spacefaring vessels. All different classes, ranging from *Colossus* to *Behemoth* and *Leviathan*, littered the bay along their respective ship slots. Their size alone made the *SnapShot* look like an ant, and the sheer number of them made it all the more intimidating. It was the largest fleet any of them had ever seen, even Chris.

The team had been instructed to dock their small, fighter-like vessel inside one of the larger *Leviathan's*, one with the title of *Moonshot.*

James swung the *SnapShot* into the bay of the UEA *Moonshot*, where many soldiers and commanders were moving about and doing their own business.

Through the front window, Chris could see Alterous and two of the other Council members waiting patiently for the team's arrival. He recognized one of them to be Jackson, the man who spoke up when they returned with the Particle Breaker.

The *SnapShot* set down gently onto the deck, and the engines whined down. Chris and the others made their way out and over to the Council members.

"Follow us," Alterous said as soon as they arrived. He turned and began walking through the bay, the rest following. They stopped outside of a set of doors that lead to an elevator. Waiting for the doors to spread, nobody spoke a word. James looked to Chris, who just shrugged in response.

The elevator doors opened, and a platoon of Homage soldiers marched out and towards their respective stations. The group took the soldiers' places in the elevator as the doors closed. It began to rise, level after level in the monstrous ship.

After two minutes rising in absolute silence, the machine dinged, and the doors opened, Alterous still leading the way out. They walked through three more identical corridors, making two lefts and a right, until they reached what seemed to be some sort of lab.

When they entered, a very relaxed and comfortable feeling washed over Chris. It had been years since he had resided in a lab, and even longer since he had done any real experiments.

It was filled with instruments of all sorts, with a data table in the center of the room. On the other side of the room from the entrance was the Particle Breaker. Just the sight of it made the experience all too surreal, and gave him a dangerous sense of déjà vu.

"Alright," Alterous finally broke the silence. "Two days ago, the rest of the Council and I drafted a message for the president of the Terra division." He pressed a tab on the data table, which projected a holographic copy of the document. As Chris' eyes flicked through the page, he could see that it outlined a basic deal.

Both divisions were getting tired of the war. Four hundred years was a long time, and now it was time to end. The Council of Earth purposed an idea: one decisive battle, to be fought on the first of the new year. One final skirmish to end it all.

"If he were to agree to these terms," Alterous continued, "he would pull all of his forces out of the Sol system and all territory that still belonged to the Homage government."

"Which he did," Lucross observed, recalling the message that played before Chris had blown up the Terran *Behemoth*.

"Exactly. We have begun making repairs to many of our vessels that had been damaged during the recent attacks. Along with that, factories from Pan and Driven have sent more ammunition, which should arrive here in just a month. We are preparing for this final assault, and we intend to win."

"That's where this comes in," Jackson said, patting his hand on Chris' creation.

"We are going to open a rift in time, as we have told you before." Alterous tapped on the data table again, and a simulation began to play. It presented the *Moonshot*, in some deserted region of space. A moment after it appeared, it shot an all too familiar beam into the darkness.

A bright flash occurred, and once cleared, was replaced with a white crack stretching vertically, just longer than the height of *Moonshot*.

"Once the new rift is open, we have installed devices on each of our latest spacecraft to harness its power and deliver said vessel to whatever point in time they choose. This device, which was crafted by our former Lead Scientist, also collects and stores the time energy, allowing them to return to the present when the time comes."

"Has this ever been tested before?" Amabel asked.

"It has. But truthfully, never on this scale."

"So let me get this straight," James started. "You're goin' t'send reinforcements to our future selves, without knowin' whether or not they'll make it through, or be able to return, and *if* they return, you're goin' to make them fight again?"

"That's correct," Jackson answered.

"How many ships are you going to send through?" Katherine spoke up.

"The remainder of our warfleet in only one thousand large variant ships. We estimate the Terran force to be around the same magnitude. Any number of extra firepower will help us, so we've decided to only send about one hundred or so."

"And if they don't make it?" Samantha cocked to Alterous.

"Then we are on our own, and the odds are against us." Alterous' eyes were stone cold, and seemed more grey than usual. He knew what he was getting them all into. "And it is because of this uncertainty that you six will remain here, in the present."

"Wait, really?" Lucross said, confused.

"Yes. Do you have a problem with that, Commander Stone?"

"No, sir," Lucross mumbled. Chris watched the simulation where ship after ship sped through the open portal in time. He grinned to himself, knowing that none of them had any idea how long it took him to develop the technology.

"I think it will work," he said, looking from Lucross to Alterous. "I've got plenty of faith left, and I'm willing to put it in this plan."

"Good." Alterous grinned back to him. "That is all for now. The *Moonshot* will be taking off soon, and will arrive at the designated rift site in three days. Until then, this lab is where you will be. Feel free to roam the ship, but try not to get lost. If you need anything, contact me. Understood?"

"Yes sir," the team said as Alterous and the other two Council members left the room. As soon as they were gone, Lucross slammed his hand on the table.

"We should be going through that rift," he scowled, staring into the still projection of the finished simulation. "We're the most talented and powerful group in the fleet. They don't know what kind of dangers are out there."

"You do have a point," Amabel reassured him, putting her hand on his shoulder. "They might need us for whatever may happen on the other side of that thing."

"But what if something were to happen to us if we were to go through?" Katherine pointed out. "Then they wouldn't have us at all."

"I never realized just how egotistical we sound until now," Chris whispered to James, who snickered in response. "It doesn't matter what we think we should do," he spoke up to everyone else. "We've been given orders, and we should follow them. The Council wants us to stay, and I'm damn sure they have their reasons."

"Chris is right," Samantha said. "Even if we wanted to do anything else, we can't. We have a long break ahead of us, but we shouldn't waste it loathing the fact that we couldn't go through."

"It's not like we won't fight. Whether we stay or go, the mission is just the same. It's the battle to end it all, and that's what we'll do."

"We'll cause the Cessation," Lucross said in response. He looked Chris in the eyes, but Chris couldn't tell if it was with pride or disdain. "Right, well, we better get settled in. I'm assuming, since we weren't given proper quarters, that we'll be sleeping in the *Snapshot*. So, if we're all done here, let's go back."

"Actually," Chris said as Lucross and the others turned to leave, "I'd like to stay here for a moment. Since I'm the science guy and all, and this is where we're stationed, I might as well get a good idea of this place."

"If you say so." The team left, walking out one by one. Katherine looked at Chris for a second before exiting like all the others.

And, just like that, Chris was alone again. Alone on a ship he didn't recognize, and with a crew and destination he knew almost nothing about.

He didn't waste any time. As soon as they were all gone, he started dinking around the materials in the room. Typing programs into computers, powering up other devices, and reorganizing things to make it more comfortable for him. He knew that Alterous chose the lab for Fireteam Alpha because it would make Chris more comfortable and help him feel at home. All Chris could do was hope that it all would work out. Among his many powers, foresight was not one of them. At least, not anymore.

Every so often, Chris would glance over to the Particle Breaker. He was trying his hardest to ignore its presence, but it couldn't be helped.

It was there, and it was staring at him. The raw, unadulterated power that it held was intimidating, even for the man who had given it that power. The device was pristine, but he still wanted to tamper and make adjustments. He was worried that if he did, it wouldn't function properly when they planned to use it. And considering the last time he 'fixed' it before its use, it caused a colossal rift to be born.

Chris had run out of things to do in the lab in a fair amount of time. Just as he set down one final instrument, an announcement broadcasted through the *Moonshot*.

"*Attention, this is First Captain Broonski. The Moonshot will be taking flight in approximately ten minutes. If you need anything, hurry and get it now. If not, then all hands to your stations.*"

"Good thing," Chris said to himself. *Better get settled in.* He walked back through the room and stood in the doorway. Turning and observing the lab again, he thought for a second about how much he felt at home. He knew it wouldn't last long. Nothing ever did.

12
10th November 2753 03:10:07

Three days felt a lot longer to Chris than they should have. Other than the lab that Alterous provided, Chris was in a very unfamiliar place.

And that place was, for lack of a better term, monstrous.

Other than the size, the place was very foreign. Chris, although having been the First Captain of the Homage military for a time, had never set foot on a *Leviathan*.

The ship was so odd, so new, and it interested Chris. Every chance he got, he would go exploring along its mile-long structures. He would move between the vehicle bay, the command center, and the lab, weaving his way through the metal hallways and rooms.

He had struck up many conversations with a large, diverse group of soldiers. These soldiers, albeit admitting they had no idea what the mission was, were still very loyal to the cause. This fact put a lot of pride in Chris.

Many of them told Chris about their individual journeys among the stars, being reassigned from one starship to the next, until it all culminated into this point.

Chris also observed, however, that the Homage military was not just diverse in terms of age and experience, but in species. He hadn't noticed before, but many of the space-faring species that fell under Homage borders had volunteered to help the cause while Chris' memory was wiped. Beforehand, they never believed that it was their fight. Their worlds were not considered part of the Homage division if they did not want to belong. They must have realized just how much the Terra division was a threat to themselves and their cultures.

Currently held up in the lab, working on a simulation of his own, Chris was interrupted by an abrupt message from Alterous.

"Christopher, it is almost time to open the new rift," Alterous was saying. "Bring the Particle Beaker up to the command deck."

"Yes sir," Chris replied, ending the transmission abruptly.

He walked over to the Particle Breaker, slowly picking it up. It was a bit heavier than he remembered, probably from all the tampering he had done to contain its power over fifty years prior. He placed the device on a cart and wheeled it out of the room, working his way through the corridors until he reached the elevator. Once the elevator arrived, he moved inside and waited.

The doors closed, and he was lifted through the ship. He glanced at the Particle Breaker again and again. The device that had sealed one of his many fates. It was still menacing in a lot of ways, but he knew it no longer had power over him.

The elevator made its familiar ding, and Chris quickly wheeled the device all the way to the command center. When he entered, Alterous and his team were waiting patiently.

"Welcome Chris," Alterous said as Chris stopped in front of everyone. "Lieutenant, what time is it?" He called to one of the soldiers along the computer-heavy wall to their left.

"It's currently 3:15, sir," one of the soldiers responded without turning around.

"Then we have no time to waste, we are late. Chris, set the device into that slot." He pointed to an empty square space on the floor. Chris hoisted up his machine and, walking over to the slot, gently placed it in. As soon as he stood up straight, the device briskly moved down and disappeared from sight.

"Where did it go?" Chris asked, worried about the integrity of the device. It wasn't exactly invulnerable.

"Do not worry. It is being moved to the very front of the ship, where it will be activated. We are not going to fire it from here." The command deck was towards the top-center of the *Moonshot*, so Chris could only nod in agreement. "Lieutenant, put me online to the local fleet."

The Lieutenant hit a few keys at the computer in front of him, and Alterous began talking.

"Ladies and gentlemen of the Homage division. My name is Sargent Alterous. I am the First Councilor of the

Council of Earth. As you know, we have been at war for over four hundred years. This war, which many have fought in diligently and with pride, has been hard on all of us. And we are losing. We have been pushed to the brink of our systems, pressed throughout the galaxy by our Terran oppressors. But now, there is hope." He paused and looked around the room.

"We have travelled here in these limited days, to an abandoned system just four lightyears away from Earth, to prove that we are still in the fight. The Terrans are tired of fighting, just as we are. They have agreed that we will have one final assault on the first of the new year, which will decide the fate of the entire galaxy. However, this has bought us some time.

"Two hundred years ago, our Lead Scientist created a system in which we could open a rift in time. I know it sounds crazy, but it is true. And today, we intend to use that technology. All of your ships have been upgraded with a device that will control the time energy that is given off. Once the rift is open, all of you will be sent in, and you will arrive on the fateful day. You will be your own reinforcements. The only requirement is: no matter the outcome, you must return within twelve hours of your arrival, before the battle ends.

"I have complete faith in all of you. Together, we have striven to reach this point, this fulcrum in the fabric of our history. This is it. If we win, it will be thanks to you. Just be careful, men. And good luck."

The transmission ended, and all the soldiers in the command center applauded. There was shouting and cheering throughout the *Moonshot*, resonating through the thick metal of the ship. The confidence and enthusiasm of the crew shocked Chris, considering the high probability of failure.

"Alright," Alterous turned to Chris and pointed to an empty seat with a monitor in front of it. "Your station is over there."

"My station?" Chris asked, confused.

"You will be opening the rift, old friend."

Chris was taken aback, not sure how to handle this revelation. He moved slowly to the seat and plopped into it. Placing his hands on the controls, he watched as the monitor booted up and linked to the Particle Breaker. He knew what to do. He had opened a rift before, but he didn't think he should be the one for the job. He was out of practice, and had been out of the picture for years.

"Begin startup, Mr. Brennan." Chris typed in the command, and the system responded that the machine was warming up.

"Warm up complete in fifteen seconds, sir." Chris watched as a diagram of the device was transitioning from a cool blue to a burning red. A notification popped up and the shading stopped. "Warm up complete." Chris moved his cursor over the activation control, waiting for Alterous' signal.

"Light it up."

"Activation in three." He could feel the sweat falling from his brow. "Two." His hands were shaking, but he maintained control. "One." *Almost there*. "Zero." He hit the activation key. "Firing sequence initiated."

The *Moonshot* began to shudder as the Particle Breaker fired.

Chris looked out the front window to see a thin, white beam of light extending from the front of the ship. It stretched further and further away until he couldn't see the end.

Then, a bright flash of light. It was blinding, brighter than any star humanity had ever discovered, and the intensity only grew. Everyone had turned away from the window, shielding their eyes from the ever-consuming brightness.

That's when the shockwave hit. The growing rift blew out a wave of gravity, which hit the fleet with an undeniable force. The *Moonshot* shifted beneath the crew's feet, and many of them were thrown onto the floor. Chris had braced himself beforehand, expecting the large blast.

As everyone recovered, the light began to die down. It faded until the soldiers could open their eyes once again. When everyone looked out the front window, they all went silent.

It was astonishing, even to Chris. Outside of the ship, about nine kilometers away, was the rift. The long, familiar bright crack stretched vertically to assume a size just larger than a *Leviathan*. Lightning struck from its edges, sending silent booms throughout the void of space. Of course, they couldn't hear it, but Chris knew the noises all too well. It was beautiful, and it was perfect.

"Activation successful," Chris announced. "Rift is open."

"Good," Alterous said quietly, staring out into the new beta rift. "Lieutenant, send a message to the fleet. They are to depart in five minutes, battle ready."

"Yes sir," the Lieutenant said, doing as he was told. He quickly finished typing up the message and sent it out. A few seconds later, the fleet of one hundred ships began moving, one by one, towards beta rift.

The first ship, a *Behemoth*, entered the rift with a bright flash, and was gone. The next ship did the same. Then, one after another, they continued.

"What do we do now?" Lucross asked Alterous.

"Us?" Alterous responded. "We wait for them to come back."

"You expect us to wait for twelve hours, for something we don't even know will work?"

"What would you have us do, Commander? Go in with them? Go and risk everything? If we lose this, we risk losing every man, woman and child. You speak to me of brainless intentions, but intentions are eddies and whorls. Would you rather the pyrrhic choice, Commander? Would you choose a new philosophy?"

"N-no sir," Lucross quickly shrank back from the unexpected aggressiveness from Alterous. Chris had not seen Alterous so mad in over one hundred years, and was slightly entertained to see him finally letting go of some stress.

"One more outburst from you and I will relieve you from your command, and you will be reassigned. I expect no more from you, Stone. Is that understood?"

"Yes sir." Chris could see one of Lucross' hands shaking behind his back, clenched into a fist. He must've been trying his hardest to hold back.

"You're all dismissed. Except for you, Brennan." The rest of the team left, James and Katherine making eye contact with Chris on their way out. Once they were gone, Alterous moved next to Chris.

"I swear, your Commander becomes more unbearable each time I see him. Where did his newfound defiance come from?"

"I'm not sure," Chris said. "I think the war really has been taking a toll on him. He's been acting different for a while now. But, he's still got that authoritative elegance that he's graced for a while. You, however, are a different story. That was an impressive display of power just now, something I haven't seen from you in many years."

"Well, he has been getting on my nerves, and I needed to put him in his place."

"I hope you didn't break him too much, Sarge," Chris joked, putting his hand on Alterous' shoulder, chuckling. Chris looked back out the window, watching as the ships continued to file in for the battle ahead.

"Think it will work?" Alterous asked, watching as well.

"I have no doubts in this plan. But the outcome isn't for me to decide. I have faith, and that's all we really need."

"You need to stop preaching one of these days."

"I'll consider it," Chris laughed. "I better get back to the team. They might be wondering where I am."

"Actually, I need you to go back to the lab. Observe beta rift, and make sure that it's stable."

"Yes sir."

"And stop calling me sir. We both know you have more authority than I ever will." Chris looked at Alterous and saw regret in him.

"I'll go there now." Chris turned and walked back down the hallway and into the elevator. He waited as it fell and made his way back to the lab. Before getting to work, he pulled open his laptop and typed in a quick new entry.

November 10, 2753,

Experiment #2 complete. New rift, beta, is now open.

-Christopher Brennan

Once he finished, he closed his laptop and went to work.

13
10th November 2753 15:01:47

The new rift was stable. At least, as far as the instruments in the *Moonshot* could detect. Its size and power remained at a constant, unlike the original. But, with how long they had planned to keep it open, he needed to keep watch on it the entire time. Until someone could take over for him, that is.

It was the only thing Chris had been doing for the previous twelve hours. He watched beta, making sure it was safe.

There wasn't too much to do. He'd adjust instruments, refocus cameras, change computer settings. He'd already hacked into the full network on *Moonshot*, but there was nothing interesting to find. Their mission log was the only thing that interested him.

Chris looked at his watch, and saw that it was almost time for the fleet to come back through beta. Or, attempt to. Chris and Alterous had their hopes, and soon it would be time to see if those hopes panned out.

He stood, stretching from the prolonged time he'd spent sitting and staring at the various monitors in the room. His job was a quiet one, and he had only seen one or two people within the time he spent in the lab.

As he stretched, the door opened and James made his way in. He sat down in the seat that Chris had just vacated, and looked around at the various screens and devices.

"You've definitely been busy," he said, looking up at Chris.

"Well it is my job," Chris replied, finishing his stretch. "What's up?"

"Bored out of my mind, really. These twelve hours have been pretty dull, and everyone else is in the same boat as I am. Figured I'd come and see what you're keeping up on."

"Well I've been done for a while. I'm just watching the rift. I was assigned to keep an eye on it, make sure it's stable."

"And is it?"

"Yes, more so than the one at Ljuska. Nothing can come through beta from the other side unless they have the devices we created."

"That's good to hear." James yawned and rubbed his eyes. "The fleet should be coming back through any minute now, yes?"

"Yep. We should probably go up to command and watch."

"I agree. You go ahead, I'll tell the rest of the team."

"Alright." They both exited the lab and parted ways. James seemed to be heading to the mess hall, leading Chris to believe that they must be eating. His stomach rumbled at the thought. He hadn't eaten the entire time he was observing beta.

Chris made quick work of the elevator, but it seemed to be going painfully slower than before. Even so, it wasn't long before it reached the command floor. As soon as the doors opened, he made his way to the command room. When he walked in, Alterous caught sight of him.

"How's beta looking?" Alterous asked as Chris came to a halt.

"As stable as it could possibly get. All the work I did after opening alpha seems to have paid off."

"That's great news. The fleet should be coming back through any second now."

"That's exactly why I came up here."

"Think we should close it after this is all done?"

"We won't have time," Chris said distantly. "The Time Piece is back on Ljuska. Even if we were to leave right now, and at full terminal velocity, we'd barely make it back in time for the last battle. And trust me, even with the reinforcements, you're going to need all the firepower you can get. We'll just have to leave it open until everything is over."

"That's not a good thing."

Just as he finished speaking, the rift began to shine brighter, catching the attention of both men and the crew. It grew until it let out a small pulse that shook the ship. Before they could look to see what was happening, another pulse rang out. And another. Each pulse came in quicker succession to the one before it, and soon it felt as though the ship was constantly vibrating. Chris heard the elevator open and looked back to see his team come stumbling out.

After almost one hundred beats, the vibrating stopped and the light died down. When everyone had regained their eyesight, they looked out the front window.

Outside of the ship, between themselves and beta, were the one hundred ships that had traveled through. They had returned. However, it wasn't a pretty sight.

The many vessels were still intact, but barely. Many of them were charred and broken, pieces of wings broken and some engines disabled, leaving them floating. Some were still glowing with the heat from various explosions across their hulls. They were all very lucky to have made it back alive.

"Get me online to them now," Alterous called to the Lieutenant as the rest of Chris' team entered the room.

"Yes sir," the Lieutenant responded, linking Alterous' comms to the fleet.

"Attention Homage fleet who have just made their return, this is Alterous. This message will serve as your one and only warning. No members of your crews are permitted to speak of any of the events you have witnessed. Speak of it among yourselves, but nobody outside of your crew. If this command is to be broken, you will all be decommissioned and sent to Mars for imprisonment. Alterous out." The Lieutenant cut the line as Alterous turned to his fellow Council members, who were sitting at a small table off to the side. "Set up an official report for the Homage media.

There's no doubt that beta is visible from many of our worlds. Tell them as much of the truth as isn't classified. Make sure our official word gets out there."

"Working on it now," Jackson said, and the two turned to computer monitors and began typing away.

"Now," he said, turning to Fireteam Alpha. "All of you will be sent for training. Work to be the best you can be, in all fields of battle. This final conflict will likely take place over many planets, as well as in the void."

"Yes sir," they resonated.

"Sir," Chris said, "what about beta? Who will be assigned to watch over it in my absence?"

"We've already begun construction on a research structure to orbit beta. We'll be moving the best scientific minds there, and they will watch over it until we can close it. The Lead Scientist has already been found. A Falkner Augustine. The son of one of the two scientists who created the Particle Breaker."

Chris' heart broke when he heard the name. He had forgotten that his partner had a son. Chris had set up a trust account and made arrangements for the child to have an easy, wonderful life. But after all this time, Chris had forgotten to check on Falkner. It comforted him to at least know that Falkner was alive, and moving in his father's footsteps.

"Understood," Chris said, relieved.

"Will that be all for us, sir?" Lucross asked.

"Yes, Commander Stone," Alterous responded quickly. "Now, you're all dismissed."

Chris and the others turned back and moved to the elevator. Inside, they were unusually quiet. They fell all the way to the ship bay, where they filed out and strutted directly to the *SnapShot*. They had a lot of training ahead of them.

<u>14</u>
31st December 2753 22:37:19

The team had just returned to the *SnapShot* from another training session when they received the announcement that they were only two hours out from the designated location for the conclusive battle.

They had been training onboard the *Moonshot* for over a month and a half, preparing for what they knew would be the most difficult mission of their lives. Chris had never faced a fleet of one thousand ships, and he wasn't sure about the duration of the conflict. It could be days before they reached a conclusion. There would be no time for rest, only fighting.

Because they were two hours out, Chris decided to take a short nap to rejuvenate himself. The door shut behind him as he entered his room and laid down.

"I'm going to be gone for a few days," Chris told Victoria reluctantly. "We're already almost there."

"You're going to be safe, right?" she asked nervously. She was always worried about him, but even she knew that he had never faced such terrible odds. It was no secret that he was in danger.

"Sis, I'm protected, remember? Nothing will hurt me, I promise."

"You better be right. If you die, I'll be stuck frozen for the rest of eternity."

"That's not going to happen," he reassured her. "I'm never going to leave you. You're the most important person in my life."

"I know." She smiled at the thought of being important. "Should I let you sleep? Your body is resting, but you'll need to be in peak mental condition as well."

"I'm sure I will be okay. Trust me."

"How could I not? You're the only person I have to trust."

They both stood up and Chris pulled her into a hug. He held onto her tightly, knowing that it might be the last chance he got to keep her close.

"So," she said, breaking the hug, "tell me about the *Moonshot*. What's a *Leviathan* like?"

"Well, it's overwhelming, to say the least. I've never been in one before this time, even when I was First Captain. I was always given the ship of my choosing, and the last one I had was custom made. One of a kind."

"How big is it?"

"About five kilometers long, with tons of levels stacked inside. It certainly earns the title of *Leviathan*." There was a faint knocking on Chris' door. *So soon?* It had only felt like he was in the dream for half an hour. "I have to go now." He pulled her in for another hug and kissed her forehead.

"Good luck, big brother." She held on tightly until he faded from her reality once again.

Chris sat straight up once he reentered the physical world, snapping to his feet and moving swiftly to the door. His body was certainly refreshed, which was just what he hoped for.

"Brennan," Lucross called from the other side of the door. "Get ready, it's time to go."

"Yes sir," Chris yelled back. He quickly threw on his combat suit, zipping it up and snapping his belt into place. He checked each pouch to make sure that he would have everything he needed for the coming fights. When he finished, he went through the door and met up with his team.

"Is this everyone?" Lucross asked as Chris joined the party. Everybody nodded in response and nervously looked at one another. "Alright, good.

"Look, guys. This is it. Everything we've stood for and fought to protect. All the people who we have sworn our lives to. This is for them. Of course, we've had our rough patches. But there is no doubt in my mind that we're going to win this thing. Together. You guys are the closest I have to a family. We've been through the thick of it, with only one another at our backs. There's not a lot to say. I'm not a very emotional person. But each of you has earned one hundred percent of my trust. And I hope to see this through with you to the end."

When Lucross finished speaking, Chris felt an unnatural amount of pity. It was rare for Lucross to show such emotion to anyone other than Amabel. Chris couldn't begin to describe the satisfaction he received from Lucross' small speech. It gave him a sense that everything would be okay. The whole team smiled while Amabel embraced him in a tight hug.

"Right, well. We better get up to the command floor. Let's move out." Lucross broke from Amabel's embrace and led them out of the *SnapShot*. They walked across the vehicle bay, where everyone was running about and making sure things were ready to go.

Chris could grasp the amount of tension in the air. He looked around the vehicle bay, observing the others as they strived to complete their tasks.

Their faces said it all. They were all terrified, many looking around nervously, shaking in their boots. He felt bad for them. At least he knew that they weren't the only ones.

He was shaking a lot more than them. His fingers twitched, and he had to focus hard just to keep himself still. Chris was supposed to be strong, but this was an entirely different situation than anything he had been through before. The other wars had never been this deadly, and the stakes had never been so high. If he were to fail now, his whole mission would have been defeated.

The implications that would cause would be impossible to imagine. The wrath would be incredible, and the world would shrink into a bleak state. It was Chris' job to prevent that from happening.

They moved into the elevator once more, where Chris had been able to memorize even the smallest details. He had begun assessing his surroundings more often so that he could build one in his dreams for Victoria to see.

"So this is it, eh?" Katherine asked nervously. "The end of the 4 Cent."

"It really is," Samantha answered her. "Hard to believe, isn't it? We've been fighting for so long."

"I'm not sure what I'm going to do once this war is over. How do we go from life on the battlefield into a normal life? After all of the things we've done?"

"We'll be remembered as heroes," Chris said thoughtfully. "For everything we've done, good or bad. The galaxy will praise us if we win."

"That's not what I want," James responded.

"It's not what any of us want."

"Let's just focus on what's in front of us," Lucross said. "We've got a job to do. Let's save the dreaming for when we're home." When he finished, they fell silent. James grabbed hold of Samantha's hand, and Amabel did the same for Lucross. They all needed someone to reassure them before what was about to happen.

Chris looked at Katherine, who had her gaze focused down at her feet. He felt sorry for her. So young and naive, and so full of hope. If the war ended badly, her spirit would be crushed into a million pieces. He didn't want to live to see that happen.

The team reached the top of the elevator shaft and filed out, heading down the corridor to the command deck. Chris knew Alterous was waiting for them.

When they walked in, he was sitting at the data table, his mind heavy with contemplation. He seemed startled when the others approached, but he quickly regained his composure and stood up to greet them.

"Good to see you all again," he smiled at them. "And for what may be the last time for a while."

"Sir," the Lieutenant spoke up, "we're coming out of Hyperspace now, entering the Secant system."

They all looked out the front window as the galaxy they knew came into view. But once the image was clear, Chris' eyes nearly popped from his skull.

"There's so many," he said, staring blankly out the front window. Thousands of cruisers and vessels were lined up, two lines on each side of the system. One Homage, the other Terran. Within the lines of starships, hundreds of thousands of fighters and bombers buzzed between, each breaking formations, only to reform into new ones. It was too much for even Chris' mind to grasp hold of. There was a uniformity to it all, but it seemed so chaotic.

The *Moonshot* shifted to join the Homage line, coming to a halt near the rear edge. Their ship was the most important, so it needed to stay away from the most danger.

Chris looked around the Secant system, where it's luminous blue sun lit twelve distinct worlds, all of which were habitable. In the days to come, Chris knew he'd spend a lot of time getting to know those planets well enough to never visit them again.

"You alright?" James said, putting a hand on Chris' shoulder and pulling him out of his trance.

"I'm good," he nodded back.

"How much longer until it is supposed to start?" Alterous asked the Lieutenant.

"Two minutes, sir," the soldier responded without turning around.

"Then we will just have to wait and see who sends the first shot. I sent a message to the entire fleet. Once the new year starts, all calls are for them to make. It's an open range."

So, they waited. They stood, watching outside the window at the other line of ships. The two minutes felt like an eternity, the tension building with each second until Chris couldn't hold himself still. His foot began to tap and his fingers began twitching once again. He couldn't regain control; he was scared shitless.

The two minutes passed, and nothing happened. It was a standstill, some sort of old western standoff on a much grander scale. Neither side wanted to make the first move and start the genocide. The first of the new year would be remembered for all the wrong reasons.

"Wait," Amabel broke the silence. "What's that?" She pointed to a region of the Terran fleet where a light began to shine bright on one of the ships. In almost an instant, it shot across the system and nailed squarely into one of the many *Behemoth* class ships in the Homage fleet. The ship seemed to implode, and Chris could almost hear the screams of the crew as their ship fell to pieces in the vacuum. He flinched when the shot impacted.

That had done it.

The thousands of ships began to break their formations and move out across the mapped system, some taking positions behind moons or debris while others went groundside on several planets. The nearly millions of fighters began zipping around the key ships, opening fire on anything foreign. Shots darted back and forth across the fleets, one ship after another taking them head on. They still pushed through.

In all the debris, Chris was sure he could make out the bodies of those who were already deceased.

"Lieutenant, commence firing," Alterous commanded. "Make sure to support any ships that need our help, but stay back from direct conflict until we've exhausted all other options."

"Yes sir," the Lieutenant began giving commands to the others in the room, who primed weapons systems across the board.

"You six, go to your ship and make way to Secant One." Chris looked towards the desolate planet and noticed seven Terran ships moving into the atmosphere. "Like a game of King of the Hill. Take out the enemy forces there, and hold until we send reinforcements. You will receive missions and intel from me as we go along. Commander?"

"Yes sir," Lucross said, saluting before turning back to the rest of them. "Let's get going, mates." They strode down the hallway towards the elevator. Chris wasn't shaking anymore, now that he had a new mission to complete.

But he couldn't help but think about how many lives were about to be lost, and how many more were annihilated in the years before.

Because this was it. The fight that was going to end it all, and Chris would make sure of that.

This was the beginning of the end.

15
1st January 2754 00:42:29

Chris was sure the planet was once very beautiful before the conflict began. Full of plant life, and many strange, yet wonderful animals. But in just half an hour, its surface had already degenerated to a wasteland.

The Terrans burned it, taking out whatever Homage forces may have already holed up on its lovely terrain.

Before they had landed, Chris watched as the trees and wildlife burned, incinerated in an act of pure cruelty. Billows of smoke began to fill the atmosphere, hiding whatever print was left of its beauty. Watching it had broken Chris.

Now, he and his team stood upon the ashes of once fertile soil. They had only just left the *SnapShot*, which was hidden in one of the large clouds of smoke.

They would use the Terrans own mistake against them.

They weren't too far from the first of seven Terran warships who had taken landfall on the now desolate planet. A *Bridge*-class carrier used to transport structures and crew to set up temporary bases for combat until an official establishment could be constructed. There were no doubts that it would be well defended, but it was nothing that they couldn't handle.

Their black combat suits kept them well hidden in the charred terrain, and the heat from its incineration clouded them from any thermal scanners. They had to wear their helmets due to the amount of ash and dust floating through the air, but it also served the purpose of improving their eyesight in the poor conditions. They each held weapons with different classes, each taking a different point in the formation.

When they caught sight of the vessel, they took up their respective positions. James and Samantha set up behind piles of rock and detritus, each wielding an S-46 Sniper Rifle to provide protective fire for when the others would assault head on. Chris held his favorite B-54, with Katherine next to him with a slightly modified variant. Amabel and Lucross held their A-22's with courage, leading in the front.

Moving in an almost triangular formation, they crept towards the ship.

Chris could barely make out the name of the ship: *Shaft of Borealis*. It had only recently landed, within a few minutes of the *SnapShot*. There was barely any time for them to set up any of their structures, the construction only just beginning as the team approached.

Lucross stopped them just outside of the camp, signaling for Chris and Katherine to split to each side, while he and Amabel would lead up the middle. The two did as told and set up just outside of enemy view.

"Move in," Lucross whispered through the comms. *"Snipers, provide cover fire. Keep your eyes peeled."*

On that note, the team moved in and opened fire on the unsuspecting crew. Many of them were caught off guard as the shots rang out through the thick, dusty atmosphere. One by one, each Terran fell, riddled with bullets. Some managed to get ahold of weapons, but their eyesight was obscured by the dusty fog. Whatever rounds did hit the team only grazed their combat suits, providing little to no damage.

The rounds from the sniper fire echoed through the air particles, ripping and whizzing past the team and piercing Terrans in vital areas. It was only a matter of time before everyone on the outside of the ship had been taken care of, their corpses littering the ground. It fit in well with the overall theme they had forced onto the planet, and was very deserving of them in Chris' opinion.

Lucross and the others gave a thumbs up to the snipers in the back, a signal that they'd be moving into the ship. James and Samantha would be left outdoors to keep watch.

They opened one of the man-sized bay doors with ease, and Lucross tossed a grenade in. First there was a shout, followed by the conclusive bang. When the team filed in, everyone in the room had been disposed of. They moved on through, not bothering to check any of the new corpses.

Entering a corridor, they took a sharp right and began following the signs to the engine room, where the Hyperdrive and main engines would be.

One sign after another, they made way towards their objective. They met very little resistance, and it was taken care of with ease. Most, if not all of the crew were outside when the assault started. Those who remained were more than likely officers and caretakers.

The team entered the engine room of the bulky ship, looking around at the boilers, batteries and drives scattered around the place. The room was devoid of life, but they didn't expect it to stay that way for much longer.

They quickly began tossing explosives around the room, behind any important machinery and at least twelve around the Hyperdrive. There weren't as many as with the *Behemoth* they had taken down on Mars, due to the size of the ship and the damage that the exploding Hyperdrive would cause.

They finished as fast as they could and vacated the room. In the hallways beyond, more soldiers and commanders stacked up to stop their invaders. They opened fire as soon as the team exited the engine room, trying to slaughter them as they dove down behind cover.

Chris took out two of what he counted to be fifteen or more enemy troops. Each member took turns firing and taking cover. They tried to make the order of appearance as random as possible, so the Terrans couldn't predict who'd pop into view next. Chris' helmet got grazed and even hit a few times, but it didn't faze him.

Soon enough, all the Terrans were dead. Chris and the others didn't waste any more time, sprinting through the rest of the compounded ship. When they reached the door they had entered through, James caught sight of them.

Chris could barely make out his silhouette as James pressed the detonation switch.

The blast was powerful, and most certainly deafening. The *Shaft of Borealis* seemed to split in two from the center of the ship where the engine room had been. The force knocked the team forward a few feet, but they managed to recover and continue their retreat before any debris could strike them. When they had reached the position of the other two members of the team, Chris looked back at the *Bridge*-class vessel.

It was in complete ruin. The dusty atmosphere around the carrier ship was glowing a bright orange from the new flames they'd birthed. The bodies of their enemies had been scattered from the force of the blast, and tons of metal debris covered the fields.

It matched the tone of the dead planet very elegantly. It was a very picturesque scene Chris promised himself he'd make sure to never forget.

Lucross led them back to the *SnapShot*, whose cover had nearly faded into the rest of the foggy air. They entered the ship and shut the doors behind them. James tossed his S-46 to the side as he jumped into the pilot's seat and started the fighter up.

"I'll find us some new cover," he announced as the ship lifted off the ground and accelerated forward.

"What's our next target?" Chris asked Lucross as they cleaned and reloaded their weapons.

"There's a *Monster*-class starship hovering a few miles out from here," he informed the team. "So don't bother taking us down, Knight. We'll be in the air for this next one."

"Plan of attack?" Amabel questioned.

"Knight will lead, of course, and I'll be at his shoulder. Everyone else needs to be on different weapons systems. Brennan, you'll man the EMP gun. Frost, you're rockets. Amabel, lasers, and Knight will be projectile turrets.

"We'll just be aiming for all of the weak structural points while Brennan knocks out their systems before managing to attack us. The EMP will only take them out for thirty seconds, so we have a small window in-between each blast to give them hell before we maneuver out of the way."

"Sounds like a plan," Samantha said.

"Let's get going," Chris said as he walked to the seat for the EMP system. He sat down and looked over the controls, flipping the system on to make sure that everything was functioning properly. The screen flickered, and the controls warmed up flawlessly, allowing Chris to adjust himself to the unfamiliar program. He had never actually manned the EMP gun before, though most of the process was automatic.

The others went to their respective positions, switching their systems on as Lucross gave James directions towards the enemy cruiser.

The ship swung to the left and began to pick up speed, shooting through the thick clouds like a bullet.

"Prepare for contact," Lucross said. It was then that the *SnapShot* burst through the edge of the dusty depression and into clean air. Once out, the *Monster* came into view.

Shots and explosives began whizzing and bursting past the *SnapShot*, many of which hit its armored hull. James pivoted the ship back and forth, doing his best to dodge the dangers thrown at them.

"Guns, open fire! Brennan, once we're in range, shut them down."

The women activated their systems, aiming their guns and pulling the trigger to fire. Chris could see their shots protruding out of the *SnapShot* and flashing towards the *Monster*, where they hit along its metal skin.

The *SnapShot* maneuvered around and around, flying up to their foe at a terrifying speed. As the distance closed between them, Chris' controls began to beep erratically. He aimed his sights towards the center of the ship, where he believed the weapon controls would be located. It was difficult to keep a clear shot due to the shifting of the ship, but he managed. At the time he thought was right, he pressed the main control switch and pulled the trigger.

A focused, invisible pulse shot out from the round-barreled gun, screaming through the air towards its intended target. When the pulse made contact, it seemed to have disappeared, a silence following it thoroughly. The enemy stopped shooting, supposedly unable to use their systems.

"Focus fire on the thrusters and contact points. We have thirty seconds." Amabel and the others focused their fire where Lucross had pointed, attempting to disable one of the two main thrusters. However, they seemed to be unable to do so as the enemy thrusted forwards and maneuvered slightly, allowing their shots to hit harmlessly on a less vital part of the *Monster*.

Soon enough, the *Monster* began firing again, numerous projectiles making contact with the hull of the *SnapShot*.

The ship shuddered under the sudden pressure, rocking and shaking with each impact. One caused the ship to almost flip 180 degrees, nearly throwing everyone out of their seats.

"What was that?" Lucross called, struggling to regain his composure.

"Our left wing has been hit," James said, flicking his eyes over the ships schematics. "Still functional, but barely holding together."

"Focus on evading. Gunners, fire when you can." When Lucross finished talking, Chris' station made an almost inaudible sound as the EMP's finished recharging. He tried to aim for the weapons system again, but the maneuvering of the ship made it difficult.

The *SnapShot* made its way towards the tail end of the *Monster*, swinging and rotating to avoid any further damage.

In the mayhem of it all, Chris couldn't do anything. The others fired away at the ship while he waited for another opportunity to cripple the enemy's weapons. He stared at the screen in front of him, his finger twitching on the trigger as he tried to wait patiently for another clear shot. The only thing he could see, however, was the stern, which was nowhere near the main weapon controls. He looked on for a second longer before spontaneously pulling the trigger.

The rest of the team was caught by surprise, and watched as the electrically charged pulse sailed through the air towards their opponent. It was difficult to keep sight of it through the madness, but Chris could see as it contacted one of the two main thrusters.

The light blue thrust disappeared in an instant, and the larger vessel slowly began to tilt onto its side. Without the second thruster, the ship would have trouble maintaining flight, and the weapon systems would have a harder time locking onto the *SnapShot*.

"Now's our chance," Chris yelled to the others.

"Fire on the other thruster. Ground those sons of bitches!"

Amabel, Katherine and Samantha set their sights on the intended target and let out a hailstorm of projectile and laser fire. Sections of the *Monsters* thruster combusted, exploding from the impact of the many oppressing forces. In just a few seconds, the damage mounted up, and the light flickered out.

The Terran ship went into free fall, sailing down towards the barren world with a treacherous velocity. Lights on its hull flashed, and escape pods were jettisoned. The gunners managed to shoot most of them out of the sky, killing those inside almost instantly. They all watched silently as the vessel connected with the dusty ground.

Explosions popped all along the ship during impact, flinging bits and pieces all over the dead surface. The smoke billowing from the *Monster* faded into the dust and ashes across the land, the air around it glowing with the flames of burning metal and fuel.

"That was good thinking, Brennan," Lucross said, giving a thumbs up to him.

"I did what first came to mind," he responded, slouching back in his seat. He was surprised that even someone like him had been able to hit the thruster. His power must have been returning faster than he predicted.

He looked down at his hand, focusing hard to feel the small amount of returned energy flowing through his body. His eyes began to feel as though they were burning through his hand. Before he realized what was happening, a shot of electricity shot out from his fist, flicking through the *SnapShot* and over to one of the central control panels. The panel ruptured to pieces, heaving sparks all over the deck below, its fractured shell clattering with them.

The ship lurched and began plummeting through the thick air, tossing the crew around the room.

"What the hell just happened!?" James said, struggling to regain and maintain control of the vessel. He pulled at the controls, trying to steer the ship into its fall. The ground was approaching fast, more detail visible through the thick smog with each second.

"Prepare for impact!" Lucross yelled, tossing himself into a seat and strapping in. The others followed suit, bracing themselves and holding onto whatever they could.

This could be it, Chris thought sullenly. *I might have just killed us.* He held onto the console in front of him as they reached the ground.

#

Chris opened his eyes, looking about the inside of the now battered *SnapShot* in a daze, the lingering fuzziness in his mind intensifying. He swished a dense liquid around in his mouth and spit it out. Blood splattered across the metal flooring. His tongue was sore and throbbing. It must have been bitten on collision.

The ship was in shambles. Wires emerged from the walls and ceiling, their panels forced off during the collision. Water dripped from exposed and damaged pipes, and the lights flickered ominously, making things visible for brief moments at a time.

The others seemed to be gaining their composure as well. Everyone except for Katherine.

Upon seeing her motionless body, Chris jumped up from his seat and ran over to her, ignoring the blasts of pain shooting through him. She was still strapped in her chair, her head dangling from her neck unconscious. Chris knelt next to her, lifting her head and pressing his fingers to her neck, looking for signs of a pulse. He felt it, but it was barely there. Spitting out more blood, he tried to shake her awake.

"Katherine!" he exclaimed, shaking her. His heart was racing as he scanned for any sign that she was alright. He felt his tongue healing rapidly; one of the many gifts his powers granted him. But at this point, he didn't want them. He said her name again and grabbed hold of her hand, which gripped onto his loosely in response.

"Is she okay?" he heard Samantha say off behind him.

"She's alive." He looked at her smooth, bright face, contrasted by the dark blood that flowed down from her forehead. She seemed to have hit her head on the console in front of her.

He could almost feel his heart breaking at the sight of her newfound vulnerability, a twinge of guilt rising within him. It was his fault.

He unlatched her harness and gently picked her up. Carrying her in his arms, he wobbled over to the medical bay, where the door slid open upon arrival. He quickly made his way to one of the beds, where he carefully placed her delicate body.

As he connected wires to her to check her vitals and help her to heal, he still tried to wrap his head around what had happened. It seemed that more of his power had returned than previously thought.

And he couldn't remember how to control it.

The others came in behind Chris, looking at their injured teammate.

"What the hell happened?" Lucross said, looking around at everyone. He seemed very suspicious, and Chris couldn't blame him. They were flying fine before their incident.

"Must have been a delayed hit," James responded, looking over schematics and scratching his head. "Diagnostics aren't showin' anythin'."

Chris wiped the blood from Katherines face, trying his best not to pitch into the conversation. It seemed that nobody had noticed his little outburst, and that's the way he wanted to keep it.

"How long do we have until the ship can be repaired?" Amabel said, patching up a wound she received on her left arm. Lucross helped her with it while James thought of an estimation, and Chris finished up cleaning Katherines wound.

"About three, maybe four hours if we rely on the ships automated repair systems," James concluded. "Even then, the SnapShot will be fragile from then on until real repairs can be made."

"That's a long time."

"What's the plan?" Samantha asked Lucross. "We can't make any sky based attacks while the ship is in repair."

"So we'll take out forces on the ground," Lucross said. "There's a lot more work to do on this dust ball."

"I honestly think we should stay with the ship," Chris chimed in. Lucross shot him a painful glance, but Chris ignored it. "They might send out scouting parties to the crash site. There's nowhere to take cover out there. In here, we're fortified."

"He has a point," James said, closing the schematics. They could hear the repair systems groan to life and get to work.

"Doesn't matter," Lucross said. "We have a mission to carry out, and limited time to do it. We can't waste it sitting in here while the Terran scum take over the planet."

"Understood."

"You," Lucross pointed at Chris. "You can stay here. Watch over Frost, and make sure nobody else enters this ship."

"Yes sir," he responded flatly. Lucross had some sort of attitude towards Chris, but he wasn't entirely sure what it was.

"Let's get going." With that, Lucross and the others exited the room to plan their next strike. Chris wasn't worried. He was sure they would be fine.

He picked up a chair that had fallen over and set it next to Katherine, sitting in it slowly as the rest of the pain in his body faded. He couldn't help but glance at her again and again. She seemed so peaceful, which gave Chris some point of comfort. She didn't have to worry about anything until she woke up.

She was lucky.

The rest of Chris' friends informed him of their departure, stocked and equipped with multiple types of weapons and other necessary tools. He wished them the best of luck, and they departed to finish what they all had started.

After they had gone, Chris left the medical bay and tuned up whatever weapons systems were still functional after their less than graceful descent.

The weapons were set on automatic, programmed to fire at any lifeform it didn't recognize as part of the crew.

Back next to Katherine, Chris tried his best to calm down. He hadn't relaxed in almost a day, and it was surely taking its toll. Not only did it strain his body and mind, but also his power. He was becoming unstable far faster than he could hope to counter.

Leaning back in his seat, he let his exhaustion fall over him. His senses dimmed and numbed, and he could feel his consciousness falling. Faster and faster, leaving behind the reality that he had forced upon himself ever since his birth. Even before then.

"I can honestly say that I don't know what to do," Chris said to Victoria, her eyes blazing as she listened intently to his tale. "I'm in a rut. I think my power is flowing back faster than I can maintain it." He laid his head onto the table, closing his eyes as he tried to grab hold of the powers he once possessed. The energy was there, but he knew that once he tapped into it, it wouldn't stop.

"When we were young, you had complete control over them," Victoria said, reminiscing on the fond memories the two shared so long ago. "What's changed between then and now?"

"Well back then, I had just crossed the threshold. The power was mine, and I knew it. I was never up to my full potential, but I knew it was there. But now, it's been so long since I've really needed to use it. It was suppressed along with my memories after the incident on *Caroline*, and has only just now kicked in."

"And it's coming back quicker than you've ever needed to handle it?"

"That's what I think."

"Do you remember how much power you had?"

"If I had to quantify it?" Chris thought hard, trying to recall just how much he could truly accomplish with his full capabilities. It had been so many years since he had done so, perhaps even too many. "I don't know. It's been too long.

"What the hell is wrong with me? This has never happened before, to anyone of my kind."

"Christopher," she grabbed hold of one of his hands, her gentle touch soothing his mind. *If only it were real.* "You'll figure this out. And you know I'm here for you if you need anything. If it were up to me, I'd say to just find a secluded place and let it all out. Tap into that power that was gifted to you. Let it flow, and find your way to becoming yourself again."

"You think I'm lost?" Chris had never considered it before now. She was right; he wasn't the same person he once was. Whether that be Chris – a member of the UEASF – or Christopher Brennan, former First Captain and chosen leader of generations.

He couldn't just abandon the experiences he had with his team and return to his former person. The passion he felt for his friends were real, whether they were made by an alter ego or not.

He remembered every experience he had, every success and failure with the team by his side. There was never any doubt of that, but now he wondered: *Who have I become?*

The concept shook him to his core. It was as if his own history had been rewritten.

Who is Christopher Brennan?

"Thank you, sis." That was all he could say. The only words that mustered up from his conflicted mind. He needed time to think alone. "I'm going to go ahead and wake up now. See if Katherine needs anything, and keep watch over the ship."

"Okay Christopher," she responded sullenly, a twinge of blue flashing in her eyes for a brief moment as he disappeared from her sight once more.

16
2nd January 2754 07:02:56

Who have I become?

It was a question long posed to many human beings, but none so unlikely as Chris. From long since deceased ancestors of millions of people on an ancient Earth, to the now hyper advanced human race.

Chris had never considered it a possibility, not in the many centuries of his life. He had always maintained a single image of himself, one of high stature. The image stood tall, powerful, calm and yet fiercely intimidating. Everything he had once been when he had arrived on the material plane.

Everything was still on the *SnapShot* as he kept watch over his friend and the ship they resided in. The automated weapons blew off occasionally, but nothing exciting would be happening anytime soon. He sat, alone with his sleeping companion, pondering that same question that his sister had placed into his mind. One that he should have been asking himself since his return.

Who have I become?

The thought shook him down to his core. Before now, even during the more peaceful times, he had never even considered himself a changed person.

He wasn't just someone who had gotten his memories back after a worrisome case of amnesia. Christopher Brennan was a completely different personality from the one his friends had gotten to know over the years. Another mind.

Two minds in the same body, fighting for control beneath his consciousness. He never noticed before, but the question pulled him further.

Who have I become?

It all made sense to him now. Everything that had happened between Ljuska and the start of this immense battle. All the conflicts between himself and his teammates, all of the changing views and feelings flowing out of him. He was oblivious to it, but now it was obvious. Chris wanted to have control again.

There was only one course of action that seemed plausible. He closed his eyes, and allowed himself to fall back beyond his consciousness.

His mind fell further and further through the dimensions of his brain, synapses sparking around him as his internal conflict drew closer to the fuzz. Further than his dream realm, and even further still he fell. Until he reached it.

It was dark. Dark, but not in a sense of the absence of light. There was nothing. No thought, no sound. A portion of his mind that was completely blank. Until *he* spoke.

"Hello?" his voice called through the void. But it wasn't coming from him. "Who are you?"

"I'm you," Christopher answered plainly, hearing his voice echo through the chasm. "I am the man you once were. The one you have forgotten. I am Christopher Brennan."

"I don't understand," the voice returned to him. "Where am I? Am I dreaming?"

"In a sense. I'm not just lost memories, as you once thought. I am a completely different consciousness. We share memories and feelings, but nothing more. In terms of personality, we are two different people in the same body."

"I don't understand." Just then, Christopher could feel his other consciousness digging through his memories. He was hesitant at first, but chose to relax and allow himself in.

"You..." the voice of Chris stuttered, "you're impossible. You're the reason I could never die? The reason I healed so fast?"

"Yes. This was my body from the start, and now I've returned."

"Then what will happen to me?"

Christopher wasn't sure how to answer that. Obviously, the person Chris once was still existed. The only way the two of them could share a body was if they were to merge into a new consciousness. Christopher's mind and traits would be dominant, but there would be one mind overall.

The process seemed to have already started, since Christopher had never noticed the struggle in power until now. Things ran in and out smoothly, consciousnesses fighting for the right without noticing.

"There is only one option that will allow the two of us to live on." He then explained to Chris the process in which they would have to endure, to which a relatively new being would emerge. One with the traits of both personalities, and who would have lived through the same experiences. They already shared feelings and memories. The only thing left was to merge their beings.

"I see," Chris responded, his voice teetering at the thought of losing his existence. "Could we not just switch out from time to time? Share our body until one of us dies?"

"It's not possible," Christopher said, shaking his head with despair. "The process has already begun. Even if we were to work it out, the struggle for power is happening subconsciously for us both. One half of a mind fighting the other. Our body, as durable as it is, would not be able to handle that intense amount of power." Chris went silent, thinking about the road that lies ahead of him. Christopher felt bad for him, a twinge of pity with a modicum of respect. The man was about to make the decision to effectively end his life.

"I would like some time to think upon this."

"It will be so, but don't strain for too long. At this rate, our time is limited."

"I understand. Thank you." Christopher could feel his other essence back off, seemingly curling up into a corner, allowing Christopher to assert dominance in the body once again.

With this, Christopher's mind flung back through the many layers it had fallen, passing everything in his mind that he had ever come to know in his long life. He rose, flying high like an angel, before finally landing back on the material plane. A new feeling buzzed through him, as though it dampened his power.

"Chris?" He jumped at the sudden, unexpected use of his name. Looking back to Katherine, he noticed that her eyes had opened, and she was staring directly at him.

"Katherine!" Chris exclaimed, standing himself up to be closer to her. "How are you feeling? Are you alright?"

"What? Yeah, yeah, I'm fine." She looked around in a confused manner before looking back at him. "What happened?"

"There was a malfunction in the systems of the ship," he lied. "We crash landed, and you hit your head. You've been out for a good three or four hours."

"Where is everyone else?" She tried to slowly sit up, struggling as pain throbbed back into her head.

"They went on to complete the mission. I stayed behind to watch over you and the *SnapShot* as it finished repairing itself."

"Is it done?"

"It should be. I don't hear the automated system running anymore." To be honest, he hadn't really been paying much attention.

Katherine slid off the bed she had been laying on, standing up with a hand on her forehead. She disconnected the wires from her body and threw them to the side. "We should probably get going, find the rest of the team and help out." She strode forward cautiously out of the med bay.

"You're right. But you take it easy, okay?" He helped support her as she walked until they reached her station again. She plopped into the chair with a thud as Chris started over to the pilot seat.

Katherine reached up and grabbed his hand before he managed to slip away.

"Thank you for staying with me," she said. Chris considered her eyes, sad but full of appreciation. The touch of their hands sent another shivering chill down his spine as it had before, but he welcomed it with wavering caution. Something about her seemed broken.

"It was the least I could do." He responded, slowly pulling his hand away.

Chris walked back to the pilot seat and sat down. He flipped a switch and started the *SnapShot's* engine.

17
2nd January 2754 10:42:09

The team was back together again, though it was a bittersweet reunion. Lucross and the others were war-weary, their eyes seemingly dead within.

For all the time Chris and Katherine had rested, their friends had been pushing on, attempting to complete the mission that, at this point, seemed impossible.

Nobody wanted to admit it before, but they had never accomplished a feat as large as clearing a planet. It took fleets, dozens of ships and thousands of soldiers.

Chris supported his team as they entered the recently repaired *SnapShot*, limping their way into its supporting structure.

"I'm not sure how much longer we can keep this up," James sighed as Chris helped him to sit. "I'm nearly too worn t'move, and this ship can't handle another firefight."

"I know," Lucross responded, fully aware of the situation. "Where the hell are those damn reinforcements we were promised?" Chris watched as Lucross wandered off into deep thought before quickly snapping back into reality. "Brennan, any word from Alterous or the rest of the fleet?"

"That has to do with us?" he inquired. "Not a word."

"Dammit."

"How much more do we have until we're done with this place?" Amabel asked her partner.

"As of now, there are three more large landing parties that we have to deal with. That's at least an army per ship."

"Then it's not possible," Samantha said, looking at everyone. "By the time we finish with one of those, more Terran craft are bound to show up."

"I know." Lucross looked down at his wrist communicator, as if waiting for Alterous' powerful voice to bellow throughout the room.

He's hopeless. I've never seen that look on his face before.

Chris was taken aback at the sudden thought that had entered his mind, but quickly concluded that it was not his own.

Rather, his other personality seemed to be observing his longtime friend. How had he learned to do such a thing?

I followed you out when you left that endless chasm in our mind. You may be the dominant personality, but I still reign some say. Don't worry, I cannot control the body. I can merely communicate and observe, nothing more.

He wasn't sure whether that fact comforted him or worried him further. There was something strange about having another entity in one's mind. No sense of isolation.

"Sir, we have new contacts slippin' in near the atmosphere," James urgently informed their leader.

"Friendlies?" Lucross asked, pushing himself out of his chair and over to James.

"Hang on...negative. Hostiles, I count fifteen ships. All of them *Gargantuan* and above." James hit a few key commands and a map of the planet came into view on the main screen, highlighted by over a dozen red dots. Lucross studied the screen for a few moments before striking its fragile surface with his fist.

"Dammit!" he exclaimed as the screen flickered in response. "What the hell are we supposed to do now?"

"The enemy must know we're the ones attacking their forces," Chris observed. "Why else send an entire fleet to quell an insertion?"

"We're out of options. That much firepower will certainly kill us." They sat in silence, weighing their options, attempting to draw out a hopeful conclusion to the madness. However, no matter how intently Chris thought, his experience in such a situation came up short.

Look at the screen again.

Chris looked back up at the screen. The highlighted ships had moved into various positions over the surface of the world, but were soon joined by almost two dozen more ships highlighted in blue. The new vessels scattered across the planet, engaging the red ones 2-1.

"Guys?" Chris said, pointing at the screen. They all turned their heads in response, slowly realizing what was taking place.

"It's about damn time!" Lucross said, bounding to his seat with renewed energy. As he placed himself, a message came in through the comms.

"*UEASF Fireteam Alpha, this is Captain Cameron Sayan of the UEA* Halon Ruin," the female voice projected through a sea of static. "*What is your status? Over.*"

"Captain Sayan, this is Commander Stone. The crew is green, but our ship can't handle another assault. Requesting immediate evac, over." Lucross dropped the comms and waited for a response.

"*Understood Commander, we're on our way.*" This news gave Chris a sense of calm. It was the first bit of good news they had received since they made landfall a day and a half earlier.

One of the blue dots began to move towards them, allowing the other ships some room to battle out against the enemy without worry. A moment later, the rumble of the larger vessel could be felt beneath Chris' feet, meaning that they were just above the *SnapShot*.

Chris and the others gathered around the front window, its cracked surface distorting the little image that could be viewed. They caught sight of the friendly *Monster*-class vessel moving towards them, relief sweeping over the team. Their promised reinforcements had arrived, and they were no longer alone.

The *Halon Ruin* positioned itself above their tiny ship, and slowly swung open one of its bay doors. James jumped into the pilot seat and started the engine, gently thrusting the *SnapShot* into the air, ascending to meet with their rescue party. The *Ruin* grew as it drew closer, more detail of its uniquely painted hull coming into view.

Intricate designs were painted all along the thick metal surface, in all fashions of reds and blues. It was a style that neither of Chris' personalities recognized, but they both developed a deep appreciation for its artistic fashion. The designs were on a level that Chris could honestly not come close to comprehending on his own. If there were to be time, he would be sure to ask Captain Sayan of its significance.

They entered the hold of the ship, the bay doors closing behind them. As they exited the damaged *SnapShot*, the *Halon Ruin* lurched abruptly.

"Where are we headed?" Lucross asked one of the crewman, who was busy assessing their beloved ship.

"We're taking you back to the *Moonshot*, sir," the man responded, never taking his gaze away from the *SnapShot*. "Direct orders from Councilman Alterous."

"Of course. About bloody time." Lucross started towards the command deck, the rest of the team falling in behind him. They moved about the hallways, never taking time to stop for anything. They made small talk on the way, but there wasn't much more to say. They were just happy to be off that dusty graveyard.

As they entered the command deck, the crew inside stood to welcome their guests. One person stood amid them all, looking the most important as she turned and saluted Lucross and the rest of them.

"Commander Stone," she said in the steady voice that had been on the comms before. "It's an honor to have you and your team on board." Lucross lazily waved his arm at her; his own little way of telling them 'at ease'.

Not one for formality anymore, is he?

Chris could do nothing but nod in response.

"What's the damage report?" Lucross asked, walking over to the onboard map of the system, which was updating in real time.

"So far?" Captain Sayan said. "Nearly equal numbers lost on both sides. It's an even fight."

"Our past reinforcements haven't shown up yet?" Lucross asked, a bit of concern and fury in his eyes.

"No sir." Sayan shrank back a little before reassuming her authoritative manner. "We haven't heard anything, unfortunately. But the tide seems to be in our favor for now."

"That doesn't mean a thing if the tide constantly changes." The team looked around at each other, a nervous gleam in their eyes. Lucross was close to losing his temper. Amabel went to grab his hand, but he pulled away sharply.

"Anyway," Chris interjected, "why has Alterous summoned us?"

"He's got another assignment for you all," the Captain said, seemingly relived to break eye contact with Lucross. "A very important one, from the sounds of it. Something vital, to be sure. You are the most talented folk in the military."

"What about the rest of the UEASF?"

"All assigned at different posts across the system," she typed in a command for the map, and four more highlighted spots appeared across the planetary system. Each one represented a fireteam of the United Earth Association Special Forces, in combat during their most demanding mission.

"Where are the others?" Samantha asked, looking over the map. "There were seven fireteams, not five."

"Fireteams Delta and Gamma were annihilated earlier this morning."

Chris tried to feel remorse for them, but it was difficult. He hadn't known much of anything about the other teams, and commonly thought that his team, Alpha, was really the only one that mattered. He knew it wasn't true. Every soldier, every life counted. But his view had been limited for the longest time.

"Ma'am," one of the crewman called out, "we're coming up to the *Moonshot* now. Should receive a visual in five."

"Good to hear," Lucross stated coldly.

Something's changing.

Chris ignored the comment. Whatever it had to say, he figured it wasn't important to their mission.

"*Moonshot* coming into view," the crewman announced. With that said, they all moved to get a better angle out of the port window. When the large *Leviathan* came into view, it wasn't pretty.

Small fighter craft were buzzing around the beast of a ship, firing shots along the thick hull. Its defenses fired almost nonstop, trying to stop the assaults and keep itself stable. The skin was sheared in numerous places, debris floating away in all directions.

"Lieutenant," Captain Sayan called, "give our lead ship a hand. Fire all weapons, send out what fighters we have available." She turned to Chris and the others. "You six, get over to that ship and get your new assignment. You're the priority, and there's no time to waste."

Chris could tell that Lucross didn't like how she assumed control over them, but he hadn't a choice under the circumstances.

They all turned and left the command center, jogging through the now very lively ship. The other crewmen were moving around frantically, running to whatever stations to which they were assigned. Once in the bay, tons of men and women jumped into their fighters and support vehicles, effectively switching on their engines and taking off without a hitch.

Reaching the *SnapShot*, which was now more repaired than it had been when they arrived on the *Halon Ruin*, they jumped inside and flew into their designated seats. James, who had resumed his position in the pilot seat, switched the engines on as fast as possible. The Captain had been right. They were the most important assets, and they needed to return to the flagship as soon as possible.

James lifted the *SnapShot* off the scratched bay deck and swung it around. The ship stuttered in place for a moment before being thrust forwards and out the bay doors.

They hadn't been able to see much before, but now it was clear. This war was taking its toll on the entire system. In just a glimpse before it cleared from view, Chris could see almost all conflicts with his enhanced vision. Firefights and skirmishes highlighting the dark void in space, all of which were illuminated by the small star at the center. The galaxy was in a state of utter turmoil, its citizens holding their breath, awaiting the conclusion that they all knew was inevitable.

The cessation of the war was upon them, and this was just its awakening.

The *SnapShot* picked up velocity, gaining speed as it soared between swarms of enemy and friendly ships alike. The occasional stray shot would pierce the fragile ship's hull every now and again, but none of the adversaries turned their full attention on the team.

The enemy ships were scattering, panicked at the sudden arrival of reinforcements for the *Leviathan*-class cruiser.

The flagship, still firing its defenses indefinitely, managed to stand its ground against the large invasion force. Things were looking on the bright side for Alterous, and for Chris.

It wasn't long before the *SnapShot* entered the *Moonshots* vehicle bay, which was almost eerily vacant. The lights shone across surfaces that would otherwise be covered in the shadow of a hulk, glimmering as if freshly polished and newly released from the factories on Pan and Driven. Scorch marks and scratches were left as reminders of what had stood in the room before, prior to their call to action.

The *SnapShot* landed roughly, its landing gear scraping against the surface of the deck as the ship shuddered. Its thrusters were only semi operational.

Chris followed Lucross and the others out of the ship, leaving it behind with a group of repairmen and engineers who were tasked with fixing it completely. The team wasted no time getting through the bay, flashing past all the crewmen left behind during the assault.

They piled into the elevator, Lucross nearly smashing the button. He tapped in the appropriate level for the command deck, and the lift jolted upwards.

There was little to no talk on the way, and it irritated Chris. Even during the pressing time they were in, a bit of conversation and comfort would be nice. Inside the lift, the team could feel it shuddering beneath their feet from the pressures of war outside. If it hadn't been such a big ship, things would have already been over.

When they heard the familiar ring at their stop, the doors opened and they poured out into the hallway beyond. Moving through, they found their way onto the command deck. The whole room was chaotic.

The command deck on the *Moonshot* was naturally larger than that of the *Halon Ruin*, with more crewmen working to keep the *Leviathan* up and running. Many of those people were calling out back and forth to one another, detailing options, events, and all other points from the skirmishing outside. Council Leader Alterous was among the center of the room, looking at a map of the system. He seemed to be deep in thought, weighing his options. It was tough running one front of a war, but he didn't step down from the task.

Upon Alphas arrival, Alterous turned away from the map and watched them walk in, a look of surprise and relief on his face. He barked a few commands to his crew, instructions to send forces to other parts of the system.

"You were fast," he said, turning to Lucross and the others. He still only gave half attention, trying to focus as much as he could on the war. He tapped a few more commands into the main console next to him. "We have a very important assignment for you. What is the condition of your craft?"

"Sir," Lucross started, "some repairs were made while on the *Halon Ruin*, but the *SnapShot* is still very fragile." Lucross kept glancing at the map projected on the holodeck in front of them.

"That can be taken care of easily. I'm sure my people have already gotten started. How are you all?"

"Very exhausted, sir. We were tasked with clearing an entire planet, after all." Chris could hear the disdain in Lucross' voice.

Can't blame him. That mission was impossible. Each of you had almost died during those assaults.

"Sir," James piped, "what is the mission that you have in store for us?"

"Well, I'm sure you all are aware that the reinforcements we sent from the past have not arrived yet." Disappointment in Alterous' voice. "And the forces on either side are being spread pretty thin. We need a way to strike a major blow against the Terrans without spending too many unnecessary resources.

"You six will take your repaired vehicle and make a jump through Hyperspace to the Terran flagship. From there, you will board the structure, execute their leader, and detonate the ship."

"Sir?"

"For now, while your ship is being repaired, you will rest in the lab you had been assigned in before. We moved some cots in there for your comfort, and the mess hall is fully operational in case you need to replenish your energy. You are all dismissed."

Silently, the team turned and began walking away, except for Chris. Instead, he approached Alterous with a stern look.

"You really think they will be able to pull that kind of stunt off?" Chris asked, waving his hand in the general direction his friends had just left in. "We have never taken down a *Leviathan* in our careers, and there is a reason for such. Why not send in a larger boarding party?"

"Because you are going to be with them, Christopher. Whether powerful or not, your presence always brings some sort of satisfying luck to those around you. Miracles are abundant when you are nearby, you know that."

"They're still ill equipped for the job. I'm sure you have an idea of just how many soldiers will be on that ship. How many of them do you think will be biologically enhanced?"

"You will all be fine."

"Sargent." Alterous looked Chris dead in the eyes when he heard his name. "We'll do what we have to." Chris turned away and began walking back to the elevators to catch up with his friends. If there were any sort of way he could help them, he would do it.

His powers were slowly coming under his control, he could feel it. The energy coursed through his veins faster than his blood ever could, but it still wasn't enough. He would never be able to control his power until he had connected both consciousness'. Until then, the power was almost pointless to be in his possession, and almost dangerous.

We'll figure something out. We always do.

"You don't know that," he whispered to himself as he entered the empty elevator. "Not this time."

Christopher, do have any idea how much pressure is being put upon me? Not only that, but it's being put there by YOU. You're asking me to give up my existence.

"If you don't, we'll all die. I won't let that happen."

You don't have a choice. We both know you can't force me into this conscious mutation. The choice is mine, and I haven't made my decision yet.

"Well make it fast." With that, Chris put a mental block between his personalities. He wasn't in the mood to chat with him.

Chris made his way out of the lift and walked himself through the familiar corridors to the lab. When he entered the room, his friends had already settled down onto their individual cots, which had been spread around the room. As Chris observed the room, the *Moonshot* still rocked with weapons fire and collisions.

He moved to the only empty sleep space, positioned between where Katherine and James were soundly sleeping. Dropping onto the makeshift bed, he slowly lowered himself down. Closing his eyes, he did his best to relax in the rocking ship. He shifted around in his combat suit, which he hadn't shed for days. And even so, it would be a while before he could wear normal clothes again.

How long will it take? He wasn't sure. But as he fell into a sound sleep, he could only hope it could be soon.

"Split personalities?" Victoria asked, a confused look flashing across her face. "How is that possible?"

"I'm not one hundred percent sure," Chris responded quietly, staring into the mug in his hands. "But I know how to fix it. The thing is, the other me isn't sure if he wants to. I don't know what else to do."

"Well, other than that. How is the war? I'm assuming good, since you found the time to sleep."

"I guess. I'm not entirely sure how to explain it. It's just kind of an equal battle on both sides." Chris paused, his mind flashing back to the encounter with Sargent. It wasn't every day that they disagreed with one another. "Alterous is planning on sending my team and I to infiltrate the Terran flagship, but I'm not so sure my friends could handle it."

"Wait, just the six of you?" she asked, her red eyes sweeping over his blue eyes wearily.

"Yes." There wasn't much more he could say about it. His team was the best, and it always had been. But they were still human, and any length of humanity was fragile to a point. "Wait, if the other personality residing in my body is human…does that mean I can be killed?" A look of horror flashed across Victoria's face when he finished talking, the red cup in her hand almost fumbling out of place.

"No way," she said softly, reaching her hand over and touching his. "That's impossible, remember? You've lived for so long, there's no way you can die."

"I'm not so sure…" There was more that he'd have liked to say, but instead he faked a yawn. He didn't want to scare her any further than he had already done. "I need to get some full sleep. I'll talk to you after the mission, okay?" He got up and moved over to her, with her taking the hint and standing as well.

They embraced once again, brother and sister in unity as he pulled his consciousness away. This hug was much longer than any of the others before, but Chris was fine with that. The last thing he saw were her burning eyes as his mind faded back into his slumbering body.

18
3rd January 2754 22:01:12

Fireteam Alpha stood with Alterous and the other present Council members on the command deck of the *Moonshot*, running over the details of the plan before their final departure. The plan had been drafted by the Councilmen before the team had arrived on the ship, and there weren't very many practical ways to change the details.

The plan sounded simple enough: approach the enemy ship at twice the speed of light, board the vessel, locate and execute the Terran President and all other important crewman thereof, and escape. However, Chris and the others knew that it would be no easy task, and that their chances of survival were very slim. But the team had a confidence that almost horrified Chris. Anyone knows that the most confident driver is also the most likely person to cause an accident.

Alterous had no intention of changing his mind, though he did seem a bit less concrete on the trust he placed in them. It had never occurred to him before that they were only human beings, and nothing more.

Chris was glad to see his old friend finding more common sense, but it was already too late.

Chris didn't know much about their target. The President of Terra, Dr. Joseph Simeon, had been elected only fifteen years before the 4 Cent War kicked off. It was he who had desperately approved of the plan to try and colonize Cleave and its inhabitants, and Chris was more than sure that Simeon had more regret in his heart than anyone else in the galaxy.

His choice caused the destruction of trillions of innocent lives.

As the others talked on about the details of the mission, Chris calmly stared out through the portside window. From the current position of the *Moonshot*, he could almost see the entire solar system. He could make out ships dashing about through the dark, blasts and explosions flashing everywhere they turn. With each, numerous lives were flared from existence. The view Chris had was beautiful, but bitter nonetheless.

When I woke up from the coma, the first thing I really wanted to do was go into space. And now, through all the terrible times we've experienced in that unforgiving void, it still calls me back.

Chris understood. When he arrived on the material plane, he had always looked up at the stars, dreaming that one day he'd be able to visit the numerous stars and planets that were gifted to the universe by the Creator. The stunning beauty of life and other natural forces were too much for Chris to handle, but he couldn't stop himself. Discovery was in his very nature, and there was no way he would ever give it up.

"Me too," Chris whispered to himself, in response to what his other self said.

"What was that, Brennan?" Lucross asked, snapping Chris back into their present situation. Everyone looked to him, wondering if he had said something important.

"Nothing, sorry. Continue." Chris was embarrassed, but didn't regret it.

If only they knew what we're going through.

"The Terran President will be located on the command deck," Alterous continued, pointing to a red dot on the diagram of the enemy *Leviathan*. "If he is anything like me, he will not leave the room if they were boarded. He will be confident, but he will not be aware of the real consequences. With the void in power of the Terran hierarchy, there will be turmoil and confusion. This will allow our remaining forces to have an advantage over them."

"Sir, what happens if the reinforcements arrive from the past durin' our mission?" James asked, looking through the diagram to pinpoint and memorize different areas that would help the team to be more efficient.

"Well then we will definitely have the advantage." Alterous smiled for the first time in days, and this made Chris smile slightly in an almost immediate response.

The other Councilmen stayed silent, letting Alterous stand as the representation of the entire Council of Earth. It was odd, and Chris could clearly see now that the structure of the government had changed dramatically since he'd left.

"Your ship has completed repairs, and is now ready to transport you to the adversary. Whenever you are ready, gather whatever supplies you may need and go ahead. You are all dismissed. Good luck." Alterous didn't wait for them to leave before turning back to the system map and barking commands to the other crewmen. Chris looked to the other Council members, who just nodded in response.

The team left the command deck without saying anything else, their minds wrapping around all the information they had been given. It would be a difficult mission, possibly the most wrenching they would ever face, but they needed to find a way to manage.

The unfortunate fact about *Leviathan*-class ships was that they were made up of tight, crowded corridors that had hundreds of different rooms. The team had never gotten used to fighting in such a claustrophobic environment, even in all their years of combat. It only made their task more stressful, but they'd make it work.

Chris and the others slowly walked down the hallway and into the elevator. Nobody said a word, and Chris knew they wouldn't until they reached the *SnapShot*.

The elevator descended, and they strode through the bay, the other members of the crew watching them intently. Apparently, they had already caught wind of what Alpha team was about to attempt and must have been concerned. They were all putting their lives and faith in the hands of just six soldiers.

He was surprised when his eyes caught sight of the *SnapShot*, the hull gleaming as if it were just factory made.

There seemed to be different attachments placed on it, as well as more weapons. He could only guess that it was upgraded technology, otherwise it wouldn't have been messed with.

I don't know whether I like the changes or not.

Chris agreed.

Lucross entered the newly refurbished vessel first, each of the others following closely behind. When they all entered, it was disorienting. The ship was almost unrecognizable on the inside. The interior was completely redone, and numerous gadgets and weapons had been placed on board. New stations were added to accommodate new systems that had been installed, and the pilot seat had been upgraded as well. They all exchanged weary looks, unsure about what they had been presented.

Without wasting any more time, the team went through each system in the ship, testing each one to make sure they worked properly. Everything seemed to be in peak condition, but only time would tell.

They next went through weapons, ammunition, and other equipment. Many of the weapons that had been loaded were newer models, outfitted completely for special operations. They were provided new helmets, each with improved and upgraded communication systems and firmware. Though they were aesthetically similar, the Heads-Up Display had been modified.

Chris and the others had moved whatever personal belongings they had onto the *Moonshot* during the

SnapShot's reparation, and figured not to bother putting it back.

Once all the systems had been checked and equipment stocked, James jumped up into his seat. He sat for a moment, hesitating before finally switching on the engine.

"Alright," Lucross said. "Let's get going." With that, James lifted the ship, swung it around and exited the vehicle bay. Back into empty space, the *SnapShot* soared through the void to the front of the *Moonshot*, looking out over the entire Secant system. "The Terran flagship is on the other end of the system. We get there, we get in, we get the job done. Take us into Hyperspace, Knight."

"Yessir," James said, flipping a few switches before pressing a button. Before long, the ships advanced Hyperdrive whined to life, and the wonderful view flicked out of focus.

"How long until we arrive?" Chris asked, grabbing a new B-63 Burst Rifle and looking it over. He was unfamiliar with the new types and models, so he figured he'd get a head start before going in blind.

"Should be about two hours at our current speed, give or take a few minutes," James said, looking over one of his many monitors. "A lot longer than I'd hoped, but we were ordered only twice light speed."

"It at least gives us time enough to prepare," Amabel said.

"She's right," Lucross said. "Do whatever you guys need to before we arrive. Eat, sleep. Whatever needs to get done." When he finished talking, they all went about their separate ways through the ship.

Chris, almost by instinct or habit, immediately went back to his room and let the door shut behind him.

Nearly two hours passed with no notable action or interaction among the *SnapShot's* crew.

Everybody seemed to be keeping to themselves. Chris had decided to take this to his advantage and have a lengthy conversation with the other consciousness residing within his mind.

He had expected a certain amount of likeness, but nothing as similar as they had become. His other personality seemed to be an exact clone of his own, molded further by the experience of other events. Chris merely had the memories of those three years of military service after the coma, but he hadn't experienced them as his other self had.

They had the same hobbies and interests, which allowed for some amount of camaraderie between the two. If he had to be honest, he really didn't mind having a partner in his head. Chris despised loneliness, despite his tendancy to be antisocial. A certain affinity was developing for his other half, and he welcomed it.

But that did not change his mind.

As soon as the conversation between the two minds ended and Chris entered reality again, Lucross called the team out to the main deck.

The plan was set in motion, and there would be no turning back.

Chris tossed himself off his bed and walked out of his barren room, leaving behind little evidence of his presence. He had his new Burst Rifle in hand, which he had inspected inside and out. It was unloaded, of course, but that would change in a matter of minutes.

He rushed into the main room along with everyone else, each member arriving at the same time.

Everyone seemed to be nervous, looking around at one another and moving various parts of their bodies in an almost synchronized rhythm, and Chris could understand why.

They're doubting themselves.

Chris wasn't surprised, of course. He had his own doubts, but none in himself. He was powerful, and they weren't. The only thing that he had stressing his mind was the possibility of his newfound mortality.

"Well," Lucross started, standing in front of his team. "This is it. If we succeed, the war will be won, and we can all go home. We're going to win it all, and our time will be over." Chris thought he could almost see a tear in Lucross' eye, but he couldn't be sure. "We all know what to do, yes?" They all nodded in response. "Good. We'll storm that ship and get that son of a bitch."

"Comin' out of Hyperspace now," James called from the pilot seat.

"Alright, everyone to your stations. There is guaranteed to be a firefight outside of that ship and we're about to jump right into it."

They ran to their designated spots, seating themselves and buckling down. The ride was about to get bumpier than a shuddering roller coaster. Chris sat at the EMP station once again, quickly adjusting the device for various ranges and powers.

Just as he finished, he looked up in time to see normal space return to view. The front window, as well as his view screen, filled with hundreds of different fighters from opposing sides. All of them whizzed around, dancing with each other as they tried again and again to run the other down.

Shots were fired on all sides of the *SnapShot*, the ship jolting and shaking wildly in response. Blasts and implosions filled the darkness with brilliant oranges and reds, fires puffing out just as quickly as they started.

Once Alpha team had entered the arena, they gained a lot of attention.

Their target – the *Leviathan*-class TDV *Hopeless Wonder* – was stationed on the other end of the field, its weapons firing nonstop at the attackers swarming around it, attempting to strike it down.

The shear amount of conflict caught the team off guard, and James veered the *SnapShot* over and around, attempting to dodge the projectiles shooting through space. The ship swerved left and right, shifting again and again, nearly forcing the crew from their seats.

Without waiting for the order, the ladies at their stations activated their weapons systems, firing out across distances to the other fighters. The view was shaking too much for

Chris to make out the results of their efforts, so he could only hope. At his own station, Chris took a shot every chance he got, frying the systems on other ships as the *SnapShot* flung itself towards the *Hopeless Wonder*.

The distance was closing fast, coming down to about 5 kilometers between the two. If it weren't for the numerous vessels thrusting in every direction, they'd have already shown up. As Chris shot, he estimated their arrival in just two more minutes.

As he contemplated this thought, the left wing of the *SnapShot* was struck by a rocket. A shockwave reverberated through the ship, and the lights began to flicker. Despite this, the *SnapShot* kept moving forward. The hull must've been upgraded, as a normal hit like that beforehand would have downed the ship in seconds.

They kept pushing through, and the distance drew shorter. Nobody said a word, but they all continued their assault.

Many ships were combusting, shooting one another again and again. It was extreme chaos, almost too much to understand clearly. It was one of the largest battles Chris had ever witnessed. In the background, the *Leviathan* loomed over the battlefield, asserting its dominance in a terrifyingly subtle way.

"Approaching the *Hopeless Wonder* now," James said as he jerked the ship to the left. "Interception in thirty seconds!" As soon as he stopped speaking, another collision rocked the *SnapShot* and it began to violently shudder.

"Dammit!" Lucross yelled over the chaotic rumbling. "Main thrusters have been hit, we're losing control!" The ship began to lurch and spin in every direction, as though it were trying to tear itself apart. It was clearly out of control.

Chris could only scarcely make out James through the madness, trying to maintain control and maneuverability over the ship, but he was having difficulty. Through the front window, the looming *Leviathan's* form was gone, and was instead replaced with the detailed hull of the large vessel. Chris closed his eyes and willed a small amount of power into the ship, helping to keep it together.

James managed to gain stability and the ship stopped spinning. As soon as he regained control, he switched off the forward thrusters. The ship was dangerously close now.

"Knight, steer us into the bay," Lucross said, pointing towards the opening in the thick hull of the *Wonder*.

"At this speed?" James questioned frustratingly, doing his best to avoid debris with the secondary thrusters.

"Now!" The *SnapShot* shifted violently at the order as James steered it roughly towards the open vehicle bay, with only seconds before impact.

As the ship swung into the bay, the left wing caught onto the frame of the bay doors. The *SnapShot* jerked forcibly as the wing snapped off with a loud *CRUNCH*, the metals and tubes smashing together before breaking apart.

Chris struggled to keep his power over the ship as the *SnapShot* thudded across the metal flooring of the bay, spinning and screeching its way through crates and smaller vessels. The dizzying spin caused enough force to break

Chris' straps and throw him around in the ship. He hit tables, chairs and the walls, each impact causing a new shot of pain. He did his best to catch himself on anything, but to no avail.

Soon, the spinning stopped and the ship smashed against the back wall of the *Leviathan's* bay. Chris fell, his body aching severely as he slumped to the floor, releasing his hold of power.

"Everybody okay?" Lucross yelled as he hoisted himself from his seat. Chris struggled slowly to pick himself up, reaching for and supporting himself on the chair next to him. As he steadied himself, he looked around the room at the scattered equipment. The ship seemed a lot worse off than it had been before, but systems still functioned. "Automate the weapon systems," he ordered. "Have the ship give us cover as we prepare to leave." Everyone entered different codes into their consoles, and the screens flashed red.

James stood from the pilot seat and stretched out. Chris stretched as well, his muscles strained from the beating he had received. He was sure bruises were already forming along the length of his skin, but he could not see them beneath his combat suit.

No matter. It'll heal soon anyway.

When the team had finally adjusted themselves, they swiftly set about gathering equipment and weapons. Chris was glad to see that none of his friends had been hurt, and better still that it hadn't been his fault.

"It's time to move," Lucross said as they gathered around, weapons and helmets in hand. The ships automated turrets fired on and off at Terran soldiers attempting to make a move on the *SnapShot*. "That entrance did a number on our ship, so we'll need to find another way home. But we'll worry about that later. Now, let's go get Doctor Simeon."

Lucross adorned his sleek helmet, and the others followed suit. Chris switched his HUD on, watching as the blue and yellow designs and characters filled the transparent glass in front of his face. The new system seemed to work well.

Once ready, the team hoisted their weapons and exited the vehicle. As they fell through the hatch, they dove to cover behind large boxes and debris as bullets riddled the area around them, Terran soldiers firing from across the bay.

The turrets on the *SnapShot* fired as the enemy soldiers came into view, but they dropped to cover before they could be hit.

Chris grappled a grenade from his belt and pulled the pin, tossing it out in the general direction of the Terrans. When it exploded, Alpha team moved closer, shooting some of their enemies on the way. When the Terrans recovered, Chris and the others fled to cover once again.

The Terran force advanced, dashing between boxes and ships to keep out of sight of the *SnapShot*. The team was shooting any chance they could, taking down one or two enemy soldiers with each short burst.

Behind you!

Turning, Chris' eyes shot open as a large crate sailed through the air at him. He jumped out of the way, catching sight of a Bio. He was mangled, one arm bending in the wrong direction and his clothing singed and smoking, blood pooling on the ground beneath him. The Bio was undoubtedly a victim of their staggering entrance into the bay.

Chris swung his B-63 up and aimed down the sights. Lining it up as quickly as he could, he pulled the trigger and sent three shots into the skull of the Terran Bio-warrior. Its body froze for a moment as its face convulsed and imploded from the force of the bullets. Chris watched the body slump heavily to the floor before turning his attention back to the other soldiers.

"*Hey,*" Samantha said over the helmet comms, "*grenades on three, in random directions.*" That said, they all plucked a grenade from their belts, holding it firmly in their hands. "*One...two...THREE!*" They simultaneously pulled the pins from their explosives and tossed them at conflicting angles towards the Terrans. One second, and six resounding explosions went off in rapid succession, flinging chunks of metal and other materials into the air.

During the explosion, the team exited their hiding places and shot down what was left of the remaining Terran forces in their way. As the team moved towards the exit, shots rang out and scattered across the walls around the door, more enemies appearing from a door at the other end of the bay. They quickly jumped through the doorway, and Lucross shot the panel next to it. The door groaned as its lock moved into place.

"It won't be long before more of them show up," Lucross said, putting pressure on the door to make sure it didn't budge. "We need to get moving. Knight?"

"This way," James said. He took point as the team fell into formation; two single file on his left and right, and Chris in the back. Chris turned every so often to make sure they weren't being tailed as they strode through the narrow hallways.

They moved briskly, following James as he led them deeper into the enemy ship. An eerie feeling fell about them. Terran territory was always dangerous.

As they moved, a burst of fire echoed through the seemingly endless hallway. A strong pitch of pain stung just above Chris' left hip. He doubled over, instinctively pressing his hand against the area of soreness. The rest of his friends returned fire as he shuffled out of the way. He pulled his blood-soaked hand away from his side and stared in agony, a small rage building inside of him.

God dammit, not again.

His blue eyes burning brighter, he grabbed hold of his weapon and channeled some of his energy into it. He flashed back up and reengaged in the fight, pointing his Burst Rifle down the corridor and opening fire on the unsuspecting soldiers.

The enemies dropped to the ground like flies, their souls pouring out of their bodies with the flow of blood. Nobody but Chris could see it, but his shots followed their victims, each one landing either in the heart or the head.

It was a nasty sight, but a necessary one. As soon as they all fell to him, he stopped his assault.

Chris looked at his team, seemingly shaken from the sudden attack. Nobody was severely injured, but Samantha's shoulder had been grazed, as well as Lucross' leg. A bullet was lodged in the chest plating of James' combat suit, but hadn't pierced all the way through.

Ouch. They're luckier than we are.

Looking down, Chris could see that his wound had not begun healing yet. The pain was building, his power flowing around rather than into it. It worsened, growing with intensity as he watched the blood flow. *Not good*, he thought. *Definitely not good.*

James helped Chris patch up the wound, feeling it sting as the battlefield medications kicked in. He flinched as it was wrapped, but managed to keep his turmoil inside of his head.

"Let's keep moving," Lucross said when Chris was patched up.

They got back into formation and moved through the corridors, facing very few points of opposition on their way to the elevator. Once inside, they started the lift. The lights flickered, and the ship rumbled due to collisions from the firefight outside. Chris wondered how long it would be before either side of the warfront crippled. They had been inside the *Hopeless Wonder* for a lot longer than intended, and the mounting pressure being set on Dr. Simeon might cause him to make drastic decisions.

We'll be fine. Just focus on holding yourself together, okay?

He was right. As long as Chris focused on the mission at hand, the sooner he'd be able to move on and complete his greater mission.

As the elevator approached their stop – the floor beneath the command deck – they each pressed to one side or the other from the door, shielding themselves for whatever dangers would be waiting for them.

When the doors slid open, a hailstorm of bullets spread through the elevator. The rounds pierced the rear end of the lift, scattering holes and lodging bullets on its otherwise clean surface. Alpha team stayed hidden, flinching as the bullets passed inches from their protected faces.

The bullets stopped firing, and everything went quiet for a moment. Footsteps could be heard approaching the doors, which seemed to stay open as the oppressors approached. When the footsteps stopped close enough, Chris pulled his CMK from his belt and swung its thin blade around the corner.

A scream emanated beyond the doors, but was quickly cut off as Chris sliced his knife through the victim it had latched to. Pulling the blade back into the elevator, the rest of the team shifted themselves into view and opened fire. Chris joined them after sheathing his CMK once more, firing normal rounds from his B-63 into the group of Terran soldiers and crewmembers.

The soldiers fell fast, and the scuffle was over within seconds. The teams new combat suits were already garnishing a war-torn look, much to Chris' dismay. Gashes in the material managed to show pale skin from the people beneath, and the integrity of the armored plating was wearing down quickly. Any more substantial amounts of pressure would surely be a final test to the structure of the attire.

The team moved through various corridors, coming across the occasional crewmen and soldier patrols.

Chris was surprised to see that his team had been able to push through so well. He knew that there had never been a Homage attack force on the *Wonder's* doorstep, the halls would most certainly be filled with more attackers than they would be able to handle.

We're lucky. Seems you've still got that power packed tight.

We'll see, Chris thought back as he continued with the others. James kept them on course, navigating them to the location they were certain Dr. Simeon would be held up.

Soon, they reached the spot located beneath the command deck. The observation deck they were in, according to the schematics, seemed to be almost the same size as the deck above it. This would prove to work in their favor.

They each pulled three explosives from their belts and, under the direction of James, placed them in vital areas around the ceiling. Each device was switched on, ready to be detonated remotely. Chris and the others jogged back down the corridor and took cover.

"Ready your weapons," Lucross said, holding the detonator close to his chest, his A-26 held firmly in his other hand. "Ready?" Everyone nodded. "In three...two....one..."

Lucross pressed the button on the detonator, and Chris held his breath.

Barely a second later, a large blast shot about the corridor, flinging shrapnel and other debris their way. Even sitting behind cover had not been enough to protect them from the force of the explosion, as they were thrown off-balance by its power.

Before the dust could settle and the team recovered, a loud, metallic groan filled the singeing air. Chris looked up just before the ceiling caved in.

Chunks of metal, consoles, chairs and other objects were scattered across the collapsing room. Chris became slightly disoriented, as if another world had fallen upon the one he was in. Regaining a sense of location, he and the others stood and rushed into the ruins. The dust and smoke masked them as they moved around the piles of rubble as fast and efficiently as they could, making sure to shoot any live members they came across.

The crew who had fallen through the flooring were completely off-beam as they tried to pick themselves up. Many had been injured during the fall; others had been killed or unconscious.

As Chris moved to shoot a young private, a Bio jumped out of a pile of scrap with a magnum in hand. Startled, Chris tried to jump out of the way, but the Bio managed to grab hold of him and yank him to the floor.

The landing was rough, Chris' back struck the coarse, jagged ground. He tried to move away from the sharp pain, but the Bio pressed him firmly against the floor.

He swung the magnum to Chris' head and pulled the trigger, the blast nearly deafening him. The force knocked his head around as he closed his eyes. When he opened them again, he saw that the bullet had lodged itself into his helmet, sitting in the shattered glass just a centimeter from his right eye.

"Chris!" he heard James yell to his right. When he tried to look, another shot sounded off. Chris flinched his eyes shut, waiting for a bullet to dig into his skull. But it never came. Opening his eyes and looking through the shattered glass of his visor, he watched as the Bio limply fell beside Chris, his face blown wide open. Katherine stood over him with her Burst Rifle, the barrel smoking.

Chris stood up and grabbed his own B-63, turning to look at Katherine.

"Thank you," he said. It was difficult to see her face through the helmet. He put his hand on her shoulder, looking through her helmet and at her eyes. Her reaction delayed, her head flicked to face Chris, her eyes brightening slightly.

"You're welcome," she responded, and moved away to the others.

Chris took off his helmet, looking at the damage from the outside. The bullet had almost penetrated completely, and the glass was fractured across it. He had been lucky, as always. Just one touch would break the glass clean through.

He tossed the helmet to the side and listened as the visor scattered to pieces. When he moved back to the others in the group, they all heard a faint coughing. Following the sound through the rubble, they walked through until they found its source.

A man was sitting among the remains of the command deck, leaning against the window at the end of the corridor. He wasn't tall, but he certainly had an atmosphere of authority about him. He wore a suit similar in style to Alterous, but pure black, and with less pins. His eyes had a terrified look, pupils dilated inside of his bright hazel iris', a gash on his forehead pouring blood over half of his face.

This man was Dr. Joseph Simeon, the President of the Terra division.

When he caught sight of Alpha team, he willed himself to stand, only to fall back to the ground. He looked up helplessly as they approached, but his demeanor didn't falter. However, when his eyes fell on Chris, they grew even more fearful.

He recognizes you.

"I had a feeling that one day…you would come for my life," he said, his voice hoarse as he took heavy, shallow breaths. "I just never assumed…it would be so soon."

Lucross approached the president, dropping his helmet and Assault Rifle and bending to pick a magnum from the floor. He positioned himself next to Simeon and pressed the gun to the defenseless man's temple.

Dr. Simeon closed his eyes slowly, but then did the opposite. He shifted his gaze from Chris to Lucross, growing more serious as they moved. When his eyes met Lucross', he spoke again.

"You really think this…makes you a winner?" he asked, a bit of fury and triumph building in his frail voice. "You take me out…and what does that…make you? You've already slaughtered…so many of my people. My blood is just another…drop in a bucket that's already…overflowing."

"Shut up," Lucross said, his eyes piercing the man sitting before him. He had a stern look on his face, ignoring his surroundings and only focusing on Simeon. "With your death, the war is over. All of this damned fighting will be done, and we will be victorious."

"You think this is…about victory?" Simeon chuckled to himself, his breathing growing heavier. "Through all this time…all this bloodshed…you think all I cared about was winning? About power?" He chuckled some more, louder than before. "That's all you…care about. I can tell. The infamous Commander…Stone, who worked so…hard to gain so much power within his…career. My death does not…guarantee your government…victory. A beast without…direction is the…most dangerous."

"Look!" Samantha exclaimed suddenly, pointing out of the window that supported Simeon.

Out in the void beyond the *Hopeless Wonder*, over one hundred ships flashed into view, each one garnishing the familiar insignia of the Homage military.

They immediately launched into combat, spreading across the system of planets like a virus to the Terrans.

"Well, looks like our reinforcements arrived after all," James sighed, placing a hand on Samantha's shoulder. Chris looked back to Simeon, whose face now bore a defeated mark, the light in his eyes fading.

"Enjoy this victory, Commander Stone," he said, his voice drawn down to a whisper. "Bathe in the power that you…crave to possess." Lucross pressed the magnum more firmly onto Dr. Simeon's temple. Simeon closed his eyes, waiting for his time to end.

Wait!

"Wait," Chris said just before Lucross could pull the trigger. Everyone turned to face him, confused at his interjection. "There's no need to kill him. He's already been defeated, whether we kill him or not won't change the outcome of the war now. Take him with us. Have him stand his forces down, and we can put him to trial for his crimes against us." Everyone around him looked at him as though he were crazy, but Chris stood confidently among them. His eyes met Lucross', who seemed to relax his arm after some thought.

Thank you. I knew you were more than they are.

"See Commander?" the president laughed proudly. He struggled his arm up and pointed at Chris with a newfound light in his eyes. "This is what a good man looks like. A trustworthy man. Brennan has more power and authority than you will ever hope to-"

BAM! Blood spattered across the clear surface behind Dr. Simeon's head, brain matter and pieces of skull raining onto the floor around him. Simeon's body slumped over, eyes wide open and darker than Chris could bear to see. A dark line of smoke emanated from the barrel of the magnum in Lucross' hand. His hand shook as he dropped the magnum at his feet.

"What the hell was that!?" Chris shouted at Lucross, who mounted his Assault Rifle onto his back once more. "He had given up. There was no reason to kill him!" Chris' hand balled into a fist as Lucross moved to avoid eye contact.

"You were both right," Lucross said coldly. "Whether he lived or died wouldn't matter in the end." *One hit to end him,* he thought. *That's all it would take.* Chris nearly took a swing at his friend, but his other consciousness willed him not to. The effort to do so caused his wounds to flare up in pain, but he ignored them. "I did the right thing."

The rest of the team was in shock, unsure of what to make of the event they had witnessed. They stayed silent, much to Chris' dismay.

"Let's get out of here," Lucross said, moving back through the debris-covered corridor. He lifted his wrist comm to his face. "Councilman Alterous, our mission is complete. The president is dead, and we'll be heading back to the *Moonshot* soon. Over."

As the others moved to follow Lucross out, Chris approached the corpse of Dr. Simeon. He bent over his deceased enemy. Letting out a long sigh, he moved Simeon's eyes shut and grabbed the nametag from the man's suit, placing it in a pouch on his belt.

The man only wanted what was best for his people. To end the overpopulation under his rule.

I'm sorry.

"It's finally over," Chris whispered to himself as he stood once more. With Simeon dead and the reinforcements arrival, victory was assured for the Homage government. The Cessation of the war had finally come upon them.

Turning to leave, he took one last look out the window of the *Hopeless Wonder* at the warring fighters and fleets. It was an image that Chris hoped to never see again.

When he began walking towards his group, loud sirens blasted through the ship, causing Chris to cover his ears from the sharp pain. The alarms rang through his body and the body of the ship. Soon, a robotic voice filled the corridor, playing over the existing alarm system, and its message was not a good one.

"*President life signature undetected,*" the voice said. "*Self-destruct sequence initiated, time: ten minutes.*"

Oh shit.

When his mind quickly processed the information, Chris dove into a sprint. He soon caught up with his teammates, who had committed to the same action. With only survival in mind, the team made their way back through the maze of hallways, running for their lives.

19
4th January 2754 01:16:33

Christopher Brennan sprinted down the corridor, red lights flashing all around him as the sirens blared and beeped continuously. His heart raced, thudding in his chest violently as his mind was realizing the potential of the situation around him.

His team didn't stop to wait for him, likely focusing more on getting themselves to safety. They were still in his sight, and he soon managed to catch up to them and match their speed. James still led, though the group was more chaotic now than they had been before.

The *Hopeless Wonder* was a large ship, making it to the bay in time would be a miracle for them.

As they ran, the *Leviathan* began to shake violently, the walls seeming to fall to pieces around them. Small explosions began to pop along the walkways and the lights, basking the team in darkness as they moved forward. The lights on his friend's helmets turned on automatically, lighting their path. Unfortunately for Chris, he had no such luxury. As he moved, he stumbled over obstacles he would have otherwise avoided, the only light to help him being the orange flicks from the exploding ship.

Don't stop! Just focus on surviving, nothing else!

There's no way we will make it out, Chris thought back. His heart beat faster, his breaths becoming shallow. Pain shot into the wound above his hip, causing him to stagger. He was soon limping, breathing deeply as he tried to maintain his speed.

He managed to keep up with the others as they made it to the elevator at the end of the maze. The ship shook more as they jumped in, throwing them off balance as Lucross hit the control for the bottom deck, where the vehicle bay was located.

As they watched the doors close, Chris flinched at the pain above his hip. He looked down and saw that blood had begun to flow from it again, the bandages soaked to a deep crimson color. It was nearly dark enough to blend with his black, battered combat suit. *Not good. I've never lost this much blood.*

The elevator started down, seemingly slower than usual. There was nothing they could do to speed it up, waiting as the ship rocked around them.

Without warning, the elevator fell from beneath their feet, entering freefall in the shaft.

Everyone grabbed hold of various parts and handles, trying to keep themselves from flinging around the small lift. Amazingly, the elevator caught on the shaft, slowing back to its previous speed. The team fell to the floor, bumping roughly into each other.

Soon, the elevator reached its destination. When the doors opened, the team leapt out and began sprinting down the corridors once again. Chris limped his way through, clutching the wound as they went.

You can do it, keep going!

His vision began to blur, and he tried to shake his head to clear it. As he did so, another sharp pain entered his right shoulder, the force of which threw him to the ground. Behind him, a small group of Terran soldiers had exited one of the rooms, guns in hand. Chris looked at his shoulder and saw that another bullet had entered his body.

Chris tried to stand, but another shot entered his lower back, causing him to cripple back to the floor. His blood was flowing more quickly, pooling beneath him as he tried to shuffle forward. Yet another shot pierced into his left shoulder, the pain flashing before he lost all feeling.

His vision was fading faster with the enhanced loss of blood, the thick, delicate liquid flowing from his many wounds. He could barely make out any of the forms in front of him.

"Chris!" James called, running back with a magnum in hand. He fired at the Terran oppressors behind Chris, managing to down two of them as they shifted to fire back on him.

"Just go," Chris responded, his voice raspy and fading as he spent almost all his energy waving his hand. James paused for a second behind cover, making eye contact with Chris. He grimaced at the thought of leaving Chris behind, but then nodded, sprinting back out with the rest of the group.

Chris sat on his knees, leaning on his senseless arms as he watched his friends disappear from limited sight. His eyes lost focus again as his enemies began to stand around him in a circular pattern. Chris tried to swing at them, but he didn't have enough energy to follow through. They easily dodged it, and one of them pushed him back down with ease. His thoughts clouded over, and he didn't move.

Why aren't they trying to escape? They're going to die, too! Damned fools!

Before he could even think to react, the Terran soldier standing in front of him pulled out another magnum, a sick smile on his face as he pressed it against the center of Chris' forehead. Chris couldn't move. He couldn't think.

The Terran spoke something in a language that Chris was unaware of, but something else had caught his fazed attention. There, standing behind the Terran soldier, was another man. He looked younger, his hair less gray than Chris' had become, and his eyes still shining a brighter blue. His smile was bright and warm, as if produced in the core of a star.

It was Chris. He nodded without saying a word, as if trying to reassure himself. Chris blinked slowly, his eyelids became heavier with each passing second. When he opened his eyes again, his copy vanished.

His Terran enemy was still speaking, remarking some sort of snide comments. Chris closed his eyes, waiting for his end. He had failed his mission, he knew that. He had failed it years ago. Now he realized his fate, and he accepted it. He was ready to return home.

Goodbye, Christopher Brennan.

As the Terran pulled the trigger, time seemed to slow itself. His eyes still closed, Chris distinctly heard each click in the weapon and felt the vibrations beneath him drag out.

A large amount of energy rushed into Chris' body. His eyes flashed open as he suddenly felt rejuvenated. This power flowed through every inch of his body, giving feeling back to his limbs. His wounds healed completely, the pain subsiding as well.

When the bullet finally entered the barrel of the magnum, it pressed into Chris' forehead. With a soft crunch, it flattened itself and fell to the floor, clattering against the metal surface. Shocked, the Terran took a step back and unloaded three more bullets into Chris' head, each experiencing the same consequences as the first.

Chris slowly raised his head to make eye contact with his enemy. When their gazes met, the Terran staggered backwards, his eyes widening with fear. Chris' irises were glowing a dark purple, his power welling up inside of him.

Lifting his arm up, Chris swung it down and slammed his fist into the floor. A shockwave erupted from the impact point and the Terran soldiers flew to the ground.

"*Self-destruct in two minutes,*" the robotic voice said over the ship comms. Chris ignored it, standing over his enemies menacingly. He balled his hands into fists, trying to hold in his growing power as it began to burst from his body. Bolts of electricity fired from his hands, piercing the walls around him. The bolts filled the hallway with a dazzling, blinding light as he lifted into the air.

He continued to stare at his enemies as the energy flung itself about him. Soon, the blasts of electricity pierced almost all the Terrans through the chest, melting their armor and burning through them. When the bolts receded, the hallway was filled with the smell of charred flesh.

The only one left alive was the man who had tried to kill him.

A smile spread across Chris' face as he stirred towards his final adversary. The Terran tried to scurry away, but the violent vibrating of the ship kept him off his feet. Each bolt Chris took seemed to shake the ship more than its destruction. Chris figured if he was going to kill the man in front of him, we would make the exit grand.

Unable to restrain his swelling power any longer, he pulled back all mental limitations and allowed it to be released in full. The bubble of energy within him popped, flowing out of his body and engulfing himself and the ship around him.

Chris blacked out, his mind falling into a state of pure ecstasy.

#

Christopher did not know where he was, nor did he care. His body felt weightless, as did his mind. It had been hundreds of years since he had felt such an overwhelming, blissful harmony.

He had descended deep into his core, his body unconscious due to its limitations on handling the release of his potential. He skipped over the dreamscape his sister was residing in, preferring to be alone after such a hardening time.

"Christopher," he heard his voice say. He turned around in the darkness to see an image of his former self, transparent to the black background.

"Hello Chris," Christopher responded, smiling warmly to himself. He was glad to see that his copy was still around. "How did you manage to find a way to stay?"

"I didn't," Chris said regretfully, his eyes trailing down to the invisible floor beneath them.

"What do you mean?" Christopher could feel a lump forming in his throat like a chunk of ice. His words barely squeaked out as a pain grew in his heart. "You're still here," he gulped. "You're still alive."

"The mutation isn't complete yet, Christopher. That sudden flush of power you felt was just the beginning. I saved enough of myself behind to do this."

"To do what?" Christopher asked worryingly.

"To say goodbye." Chris' form approached Christopher. It became more apparent to Christopher that his copy was fading fast.

"You know," Chris continued, stopping just a meter away from Christopher, "life is just fantastic, isn't it? Sure, it's not all dashing about and having adventures, but existence…the feeling of being alive. That was the grandest part of it all." Christopher could feel tears welling up in his eyes, though he didn't know whether or not they were physical. "You know what my favorite part was? Just the feeling of exploration.

"When I approached Ljuska for the first time, my heart raced. The idea of standing on a planet that orbited my favorite cosmic powerhouse was just incredible. It was a dream come true for me, as I'm sure it was for you.

"Whether I was just a copy of you or not, I like to take pride in knowing that I became my own man. I was molded by the experiences I made and the relationships I built, though my base was built on you. But I could only imagine what it would truly be like to be you." A tear began to fall from both personalities eyes, sliding down their faces as they dripped below. Chris was still smiling, but Christopher couldn't will himself to do so. He had only just drawn close to his mental counterpart, and now he was being left behind. It was only a matter of time.

"Christopher," Chris lowered his voice. "You're an amazing person, with an even more amazing task at hand. It would have been an honor to continue this journey with you, my friend." Chris began to back away, his image fading more.

"Wait!" Christopher exclaimed, reaching out and grabbing Chris' hand. "You can't leave now. There has to be a way to save you!"

"I am saved, Christopher. I was saved from the beginning. If it weren't for you, I wouldn't have come into existence. I appreciate you more than you really understand." Christopher sniffed, his eyes swelling. It was because of him that Chris had to die. Chris reached and grabbed

Christopher's other hand, the two holding each other in the endless space. "Don't worry. I won't be gone for good. A part of me will always live on in you, just as you had to live on in me for a time.

"Thank you for everything, Christopher Brennan. I hope life becomes everything you set out for it to be.

"Goodbye, Christopher."

Chris faded from Christopher's view, dissipating into the darkness that they had once shared. Christopher stood frozen, his arms still outstretched as if Chris was still with him, begging to be pulled back.

After a time, his arms slowly fell to his sides. He lowered his head and closed his eyes, sobbing as he grieved the loss of his newfound companion.

For the first time since his return, Christopher Brennan was truly alone.

#

When Chris finally found the will and courage to wake up, he found himself in the medical bay of the *Moonshot*.

As he arose, he merely sat for hours, thinking on the events that had transpired. He was alone at first, but it didn't last long. His friends came in after a few minutes, along with Alterous. He was glad to see that they had made it off the *Hopeless Wonder*.

When they arrived, Chris made note that the ship was no longer in combat. The *Moonshot* was floating peacefully.

Chris went to stand up as they were approaching, but his legs nearly buckled beneath him under his weight.

Instead, he sat on the edge of the medical bed, watching as his compatriots made their way to him.

"How are you feeling?" Alterous asked when they arrived. He looked over Chris' vitals, which he knew to be fine.

"Other than the lack of physical strength?" Chris chided. "Better than ever." He looked down at his hand, flexing it into a fist. The energy inside of him surged, causing him to crack a small grin. However, the grin faded as he recalled the sacrifice made to give it back to him. "What happened?"

"Soon after the hundred ships from the past came to our aid, the Terran flagship self-destructed earlier than its countdown had led everyone onboard to believe."

"We almost didn't make it out alive," Lucross interjected. He had bags under his eyes, and Chris assumed he hadn't slept since then. "We hijacked a Terran ship before it took off."

"Yes," Alterous continued. "The explosion engulfed most of the Terran fighters outside the ship's hull. As we approached the wreckage, your teammates insisted that we search for you. You were found floating among the debris, your combat suit in disrepair. You were barely alive when we pulled you in." Alterous looked Chris dead in the eyes, giving him a subtle eyebrow raise before he turned back to the others.

"Your wounds have completely healed," Amabel said. "And surprisingly fast, at that."

"How long was I asleep?" Chris asked.

"Two days," James said. "You had us worried, man."

"Well," Alterous said as he began to walk away from the group. "I will let you all catch up. I expect a full report of your viewpoint of the events by tomorrow, Brennan."

"Understood, sir." With that, Alterous exited the medical bay, leaving Chris alone with his friends. His heart was lifted at the sight of them. But even as he had their company, he still felt isolated. Having a companion residing in one's head was a unique experience. It was more intimate.

"So," Lucross continued without wasting time, "what happened in there?" Chris thought on it, wondering how he could convey what happened in a way that wouldn't spook them in any way.

"I don't remember," Chris lied, deciding to keep his identity and mental struggle a secret from then on. "It was a traumatic experience. The last thing I remember was telling James to leave me behind." Chris' voice was still and cold. He knew it was, he didn't try to hide it from them. He wouldn't hide his pain.

"How did you survive that explosion?" Lucross asked again, his voice growing more agitated. Chris leaned forward, staring him dead in the eyes.

"I don't know." He never raised his voice. They continued to glare at one another, sizing one another up. Chris cared deeply for his teammates, but Lucross was getting out of hand. He was crossing lines that should never have needed to be drawn.

"Honey," Amabel finally interrupted, grabbing hold of Lucross' hand. "Let's go get some rest, we haven't slept in days. We could all use it." Lucross didn't say another word as she led him away and out of the medical bay. Samantha followed shortly after, complaining that she was tired as well.

Katherine and James stayed behind with Chris.

"We really were worried about you, Chris," Katherine said, leaning in and giving him a hug. He accepted it warmly, but grunted from the pressure as his body was still exhausted.

"I'm really sorry I left you behind," James said, his eyes looking fragile. "There had t'be something I could have done."

"Don't apologize," Chris said, smiling. "You guys did everything you could. You made it away safely, and that's all that matters to me." It was then that Chris noticed that James' right shoulder was bandaged up, as well as Katherine's left thigh. "Looks like we all took some hits on the way out."

"We're just glad that you're alive," Katherine said. "I don't know what would have happened if you had died…"

"You'll never have to find out," he reassured her. "So it's really over, huh? The 4 Cent War, centuries of fighting across numerous systems, finally concluded here. With us." It was hard to believe, and the fact had taken a while to become concrete in his mind. Nearly half of his life had been spent during conflict, and the other half making attempts to complete his lifelong goal.

"It's over, man," James said confidently. "We won the war. I can only imagine the look on Sam's face when we finally get t'go home." It was at a time like this where Chris longed for a comment from his companion. Sadly, it never came.

"Well if you guys don't mind, I'd actually like to be alone for now."

He laid back down on the bed, his mind starting to wander before his friends had even left his side. Katherine hugged him one more time, and James pat him on the shoulder. As they went to exit, Chris turned over and closed his eyes.

As he rested, he let himself feel the power flowing smoothly through his veins. He finally had it under control, and was glad that he had received it once again.

Nodding into sleep, Chris swore to himself that he would always use his power for the best intentions.

<u>20</u>
15th January 2754 06:31:47

It felt odd to be back on Earth after so long without having the nagging feeling of paranoia. It was peaceful on the rocky surface, and the skies were clear of all adversity. Parties and celebrations were thrown in multiple cities after the Cessation, citizens both relieved and ecstatic about the positive outcome.

For the first time in over fifty years, Chris returned to his home in Phoenix, Arizona. It had gathered dust over the years of misuse, but he was glad to see it was still standing.

He spent his first two days cleaning up, reinstating his ownership of the property. In the dreamscape, the house remained as it was, no matter how things changed in the real world. Once he settled, he relaxed.

It had been so long since he had seen a peaceful time. He knew he only had twenty days of leave, so he was making sure to spend it wisely. He spent it reading, writing, and enjoying time with his sister.

Now, he stood in his dream, telling her what had happened between him and his other personality. The loss of himself had created a lot of stress as the mutation came to a close.

"My mind is different," Chris said, trying to describe himself to his sister. She sat still, content and watchful, listening to his words with her full attention. "It's hard to explain how. My feelings towards others and some events have morphed slightly, but I'm otherwise moving on as the same old Christopher Brennan you have come to know and love. It will take me a while to sort some of these feelings out, but I'm otherwise feeling great."

"I see," Victoria said, her mind running through all the information he had shared with her. "I can tell that you're the same man, and I have no problem with that. All of these events must have been hard on you, I'm sure." Her red eyes filled with concern, though her face didn't move to convey the same feeling.

"It has been hard," he admitted. "After having someone in my head for so long, I've just…felt empty. Alone. I needed time to think and recover emotionally. That's why I was gone for so long." He did feel bad for abandoning her, but it couldn't be helped.

"It's okay, Christopher. You're my brother and I love you no matter what. Okay?" She smiled, and Chris couldn't hold back from returning it.

"I love you too, sis. Thank you for being here for me."

"I don't exactly have a choice," she laughed. *Oh damn…*

"I'm going to keep my promise. You know that, right?" So much had happened since the final battle had started, he had forgotten about his promise to retrieve her and wake her up.

"I know you are, and I can't wait. I'm so excited, I haven't been awake in years!" She exclaimed, leaning back in her seat and smiling to herself. "I can just imagine feeling the sun on my skin and the air in my lungs. I'm ready to live again, Christopher."

"Well, now that peace has fallen on the galaxy once again, you can do all those things and more. The danger is gone. I'll be sure to ask Alterous the next time I see him, okay?"

"Okay Christopher," she said, a smile glued to her face.

"I only have about ten more days left of leave before I have to return to my team." When he finished talking, an alarm went off in his room, signaling that it was time for him to rise.

"Damn. Well, I'll see you later tonight, yes brother?" Her eyes brightened to a shade of orange he could only describe as heavenly. Chris was glad to see that Victoria was still happy and healthy, despite her extended periods of isolation. Most other people would have gone insane by the time they had been woken up.

"Yes ma'am, you will." They both stood up and hugged as always, enjoying the company of one another.

When Chris woke up, he merely laid on his bed for an hour, thinking to himself about what his future could be like.

There were many possibilities, none of which he could predict. The only thing he could reassure himself of was that no conflict would befall the Homage division for some time.

At around 8a.m., Chris finally rose from his bed and went about his house. He didn't bother to eat breakfast, not feeling an appetite worth satisfying. Instead, he got dressed and walked straight into his office, sitting in the soft black chair by his desk.

He opened his laptop and signed in, checking to see if anything important had shown up. Seeing nothing notable or worth his time, he shut the computer down and set it aside. He looked through a stack of books on his desk and pulled from it one of his favorites: *The Tragedy of Julius Caesar*.

The play had been one of his favorites when growing up, and he remembered the first time he had studied William Shakespeare in school. Chris had memorized every line of the play, as well as other works, and could recite them faithfully. Literature had once been a fond passion of his.

He flipped the book open and began to read, imagining the events described as they might have been portrayed. The part that always stuck out to him the most was the betrayal of Caesar by his friend Brutus, and the whirlwind of events that followed.

It was beautifully portrayed by Shakespeare's writing, and always prompted deep thoughts within Chris' mind.

Chris read through the play from beginning to end, with no breaks between. Some parts were read aloud, others softly spoken as he performed the play in his head. He knew that if he ever had the chance of being a part of a performance of *Julius Caesar*, he would play the title character.

When he finished reading, he set the book down and opened his laptop once again, checking to see if anything had happened.

To be honest with himself, he was feeling quite bored with his new lifestyle. He appreciated the peace, but there was still something nagging at the back of his mind.

A part of him seeking adventure.

When he signed back into his computer, a message sprang up from the Council of Earth. More specifically, Sargent Alterous. Chris opened it with delight, smiling as he read the message aloud.

> *"Christopher Brennan,*
> *You and the other members of your team have been invited to the official Homage celebration of the Cessation, to be held on the planet Ka Hale in five days. The celebration will span the globe, and you six will be the guests of honor.*
>
> *On another note: you and I should get together sometime to reacquaint ourselves. It has been a long time since we spent a day together as friends. Until then, I look forward to working with you once more. See you at the celebration!*
>
> *Your friend,*
> *First Councilor Sargent Alterous"*

Chris decided it would be best not to respond, and instead surprise everyone with his arrival. He wasn't known to be much of a socialite, but he didn't mind a good party every now and again. And with such a reason for celebration, how could he refuse?

With the message came an address and instructions, which Chris saved and sent to his wrist communicator.

In a split decision, Chris decided to leave that very day. Taking a personal spacecraft stored in a garage beneath his house, he took off from Earth and set a course for Ka Hale. It would be a three-day trip to reach the planet at the top speed of his older Hyperdrive, but he was fine with that. The theme of isolation would carry with him during that time, whether he was to stay home or not.

There wasn't much to do during the trip, so he spent his time reading through his old journal entries on his laptop. There was no real reason as to why, he just learned to like reflecting on the past. It was a habit.

He informed Victoria of his decision the next time he slept. She was happy to hear that he would be entering a social spotlight and said that he and his team really did deserve the praise. They ended the war, after all! Chris wasn't so sure he really deserved praise, but he would welcome it nonetheless.

The days were short, as he spent most of his time sleeping and spending much needed time with his sister. Before he knew it, an alarm went off in his ship telling him that he had arrived on Ka Hale.

Following the directions he had been given, Chris found himself at a Homage/Ka Hale joint military base. Per the instructions, he manually landed his craft inside of a hangar on the far side of the seven-mile base after obtaining clearance. He exited the vehicle and was escorted to an apartment complex, where he and his team would be staying covertly out of the eye of the public until the celebration.

When he entered the complex, his eyes brightened as he saw his team waiting next to the front desk. A shining smile appeared on his face as he approached them. When they caught sight of him, they all smiled back.

James greeted him first, shaking his hand, followed by a hug from Katherine. Simple greetings were given from the rest, but he didn't expect much more.

They were his family, after all.

For a moment, Chris and Lucross made eye contact. Before anything could be said, and as Chris prepared for Lucross' recently newfound attitude, he was surprised to receive a gentle smile from his superior. Lucross turned away before Chris could return the gesture, but it was enough to lift Chris' spirit higher.

As they walked to their temporary apartment, Chris noticed that Lucross once again had an elegance about him, something that had been missing for months since the journey to Ljuska. The team was happier than they had ever been now that the burden of war had been lifted.

In the apartment, they bundled down and relaxed, spreading around the unusually large living space. It was odd for Chris to see his friends so relaxed. It was almost out of character, which made him slightly uncomfortable.

They didn't talk much, which was surprising at first. But as they settled in, Chris realized that they all had jetlag and were exhausted. After watching some sort of show on television, they all went into their individual rooms and passed out.

When Chris went to sleep, he spent more time with Victoria.

The following morning, they were all woken early by a knock at the door. The celebration was just a day away, and the team was to be informed of security details and would be shown around. They were given a syllabus with details on when certain events would take place, and what their role would be in the whole shebang.

It wasn't long before they were escorted to an empty hangar, which was decorated from bottom to top in multicolored materials. Supposedly, the celebration would begin there and be televised to other cities on the planet, where other celebrations would be held.

There would be fifteen overall, with the entire party lasting a full twenty-four hours.

The team would be escorted to each city before the final hour passed, ensuring that everyone on the planet had a chance to see their "heroes" in person.

It made Chris uncomfortable to be referred to as a hero, but he rolled with it.

He had to admit, his anticipation was growing for the event. Sure enough, it would be the largest celebration ever held in human history, and he would be at the center of it all. Such a thing was rare for Chris, as appreciation for his achievements had never really come into fruition during his early years on Earth. It was only a matter of time before that became a normality once again, so he had developed full intentions of taking advantage of this praise.

Chris and the others were given a presentation on the schedule and flight plan for their day during the celebration. They were ensured that they would have a very interactive experience, and that due to the cultural diversity among the people of Ka Hale, each city will be different from the one before it.

This variety would lead to minimal amounts of boredom. Luckily for Alpha team, they had plenty of experience with exciting environments. To them, it would be another walk in the park.

The presentations and details of security took up over half of the day. At the end of it, Chris asked an officer when they were to expect Alterous to show up. The officer informed him that Alterous wouldn't arrive until the evening.

With only half a day until the party, the group of friends decided to do some sightseeing. They had never been to Ka Hale before, so the world seemed very alien to them.

The structures of Ka Hale were rounded and sleek, representing more of an advanced and diverse culture. Before humanity had spread among the galaxy, Ka Hale was populated by an anthropomorphic species known as the Safar. These blue and green creatures had a peaceful existence with humanity, with the bond only increasing.

Ka Hale was special in more than one regard. It was also one of the only planets in the Homage division authorized to have a personal militarized force. Personal security was part of the Safar culture, as they did not want to rely on another species to protect them in full. An agreement had been made between the Council of Earth and the Safar leader to allow Homage forces to be stationed on the planet.

Although Chris had never visited, his current presence cemented this planet as one of his favorite places in the galaxy.

The team was only permitted to tour the nearest city, Covern. It was a very modern city with a flourishing population of humans and Safar. Some of the buildings had a more human look to them, and others had mixed characteristics of both styles. This mix was artfully done, and very pleasing to the eye.

They visited museums and learned the full history of the Safar civilization, as well as visited various monuments around the town. Statues of historical figures and famous ships. It was only a matter of time before evening approached and they were escorted back to the apartment.

As they approached the building, Chris looked up and was surprised to see the *Moonshot* looming above the base. The *Leviathan* was shining in the dying wave of sunlight as smaller transport vessels buzzed to and from their hive.

Entering the building, Alterous was seen at the front desk, signing into his temporary apartment. He smiled when he caught sight of the team. When they approached, he turned and saluted to them, with the team returning the formal gesture.

"It is nice to see you all again," Alterous said, relaxing after the salute. "I hope you have found some comfort here."

"More than we expected to, sir," Lucross responded with a smile.

"That is good. I'm sure you know that I will be accompanying you all during the celebration?"

"Yes sir. Why is that, exactly? You're a lot more important than we are." Lucross was right. It was odd for a Council member to be out in such a public occasion, and Chris had never known Alterous to be much of a socialite. It was then that Chris realized that most of the extreme security detail was meant for his old friend, not himself.

"Son, I have been working during this war for three hundred years," Alterous said, taking some pride in the fact that he had survived for so long. "I think I deserve to have some fun at this celebration. It was my idea, after all."

"It was a good decision," Samantha said, "in my opinion."

"I agree," Katherine said, her eyes almost shining as bright as her smile. "I'm so excited for this! It's been years since I've been to a good party." She bounced up and down delightfully, giggling as she thought of the fun they would have.

"I'm sure we're all excited, Kat," Chris said, smiling back at her. Her innocence never failed to amuse him, despite her being the age of 91. "Even I'm excited, and I'm typically not a fan of these social events."

"We should all get rest now," Alterous said, grabbing his belongings from the floor. "The party starts at midnight, remember?"

"Right," James agreed, yawning loudly. "We should get some sleep."

"I will see you all at midnight, then." Alterous walked towards his apartment on the other side of the complex. As he walked away, the team turned and walked to their own.

Inside the apartment, they didn't waste any time. They quickly set alarms and fell asleep, their hearts beating with anticipation of the entertainment and recreation of the following day.

Chris didn't spend much time in his dreamscape, knowing he would need to be fully rested for the activities he would be partaking in.

Victoria was highly excited for Chris. She knew well that he never had enough fun in his life, despite his recurrent escapades through space. All she wanted was for Chris to be happy, and this was the perfect way for him to do so.

"Will we go to parties once you wake me up?" she asked, clasping her hands together excitedly. "It's been so long since I have been to a decent dance."

"I'll be sure to throw you the largest party imaginable once you're awake," he guaranteed her, smiling. "Though, parties nowadays are not how you remember them. They're drastically larger and louder."

"I'm sure I'll manage, thank you."

They didn't have enough time to talk about much else, as the moment to wake up was close at hand.

The team and Alterous were transported to a hangar in the center of the base, where it was closed to the rest of the world.

They were dressed in their new combat suits, considering it their most formal and recognizable attire. If they were to be praised as heroes, they might as well dress like it. Chris hoped it would give the crowd a sense a realism, to allow them to see their saviors were nothing more than soldiers.

To Chris, there was no difference between the two.

As they stood in the main section of the hangar, the ground seemed to softly tremble beneath their feet. Chris' heart began to race as he anticipated the attention he was about to receive. He looked to Alterous, who also seemed to be tapping in fingers nervously.

Fireteam Alpha talked amongst themselves, standing on a platform in the center of the hangar. Just as Chris was about to say something to Katherine, a booming voice echoed through.

"What is up, Ka Hale?" the feminine voice yelled, amplified many times by a wide speaker system. She could be heard clearly through the closed hangar doors. "Today, we begin the official Homage celebration for the end of the 4 Cent War! The largest war in human history, which took the lives of so many of our brothers and sisters.

"But today, we celebrate in their honor! We have very special guests for you all today." Chris' heart raced faster. "The most influential and magnificent group of people this galaxy has ever seen. They invaded the Terran flagship and made the Terran president pay for his crimes! They defended so many of us time and time again, when we had done nothing to deserve their charity!

"Today, we bring you the strongest team in the United Earth Association Special Forces Division...FIRETEAM ALPHA!"

The crowds roared in response as the doors began to open. It was as though an earthquake had been rummaging its way through the ground.

The voices grew stronger as the doors finished opening. Once they were wide, Chris' heart fell to his feet.

Thousands upon thousands of people were gathered outside of the hangar, jumping around and cheering as the team came into view. They were like hundreds of wild animals, a herd of indistinguishable faces praising the team for their accomplishment.

Fireworks lit up across the sky of Ka Hale, crashing loudly through the well-spoken air. Lights shone across the land in all assorted colors, from pinks to blues and yellows. The military base was unrecognizable, with many stations and activities set up all around the streets and airfields.

Chris flinched as each firework went off with a bang. He didn't understand why, so he did his best to ignore it.

"And now, we will have a couple of words from a very special and important individual," the announcer said. "I present to you, First Councilor of the Council of Earth, Mr. Sargent Alterous!"

The crowd cheered more as the microphone was handed to Alterous, who took it from the announcer with a smile.

"Well," Alterous started. "There's not much more to say, is there? It's been a long, bitter time for all of us, both young and old. So I say, let's make the end a sweet one." He glanced over to the team, who all smiled back happily in response. The crowd was cheering louder than before, instruments playing in the distance and carrying the voices through the sea of bodies.

Looking back to the crowd, his eyes flashing with excitement, Alterous only said two more words: "Let's go!"

Fireworks dashed about through the air and lights flashed all around as the celebration began. The crowd cheered and music blasted all along the base, swinging its melodies between the active bodies.

Chris and the others were moved through the edge of the crowd, surrounded by security, where tons of people tried to catch their attention. Everyone had phones or cameras in their hands, trying to snap a shot of the team during their "big event". Everyone made an attempt to greet them. Many hands were shaken, but Chris could hardly keep track of the faces they belonged to.

The lights were a delight to Chris' eyes, and the music seemed almost pleasantly alien. It wasn't long before each member of Alpha had split off from one another.

Chris found himself at a game station, throwing rings at bottles and shooting at plastic animals. He aced each activity he had been introduced to and had a drink between each one. The crowds of people continued to cheer for him, and he gladly accepted their praises.

He had made a lap around the base before an hour had passed, participating in games and dances.

Hundreds of people had been acquainted with him, and he could tell it was one of the better moments of their lives.

The people of Ka Hale were a friendly kind, and Chris found himself falling in love with the shared cultures of the Safar and humanity. The Safar were friendly and respectful, yet less sophisticated than the party animals they were sharing their experiences with.

When he completed his lap, security herded Chris and his team to an air shuttle.

Alpha team gave one more goodbye to the large crowds, saluting them before moving on to the next city. They each hurried into the shuttle and left the base behind.

The air shuttle was small, making it more nimble as it soared through the air. There was very little time to talk as they approached the next city they would continue to celebrate in. It was a five-minute flight before they touched down.

Fireworks and music were already vibrating through the air when they landed, the celebration having started for those citizens before the team arrived.

Chris and the others were welcomed with hospitality and open arms, something he was glad to see. He made sure to talk to as many of them as he could, sure that his interaction would be the highlight of their day.

The parties were similar for each following city, with slight variations in food and etiquette due to the abundance of cultures. Chris was adamant in acquiring knowledge of each one, familiarizing himself with the people he was sworn to protect.

In the ninth city – Ferida – Chris and the rest of Alpha team had decided to take a temporary residence in a large club, where hundreds of people had crammed themselves in to party with their "heroes".

Chris was at the bar, tossing back drink after drink as he amused others by his inability to get intoxicated. He was surrounded by almost twenty people, each with a drink in their hand and a smile on their faces. The rest of his team was spread around the club, minding their own as they went about the crowds.

It wasn't much longer before it was announced that the team needed to move on.

They regrouped and headed back into the streets of Ferida, climbing into the long limousine they had been escorted in throughout the time in the city. Inside, Chris let out a long sigh as a smile spread across his face. He looked around at his friends, who seemed to have the same thoughts in mind.

"An incredibly exhausting day," he said, stirring the others from their drifting. "Don't you all think so?"

"I've never had this much fun in my life," Lucross admitted, grabbing hold of Amabel's hand.

"A lifetime of war will do that to you," Samantha said, laying her head back. "This day is amazing. There are no other words to describe it." She looked at James, who seemed to be falling asleep as the limo rolled on.

"I must admit, I've never seen any of you this calm before," Katherine said, looking around at them with compassion in her eyes. As her gaze met Chris', his eyes shied away from hers for a reason which he could not decipher.

The group was silent for the rest of the ride, resting from the hours of activity. To Chris, it was almost more exhausting than a skirmish of war.

When the limo rolled up to the shuttle, a crowd had gathered around the large vessel to see them off. The team exited the car with smiles on their faces, playing into what the crowds wanted. The many civilians cheered as they walked through.

Chris heard a loud crack as they maneuvered halfway through the congregation, jumping at the sound and quickly shutting his eyes. When he opened them again, he scarcely caught sight of a bullet piercing through Lucross' chest and his body crashed to the ground.

People screamed as Amabel and the security team rushed to Lucross' body, lying still in a growing pool of his own blood.

<u>21</u>
22nd January 2754 04:03:21

"I can't believe it," Amabel said faintly, tears flowing slowly from her dim eyes. She couldn't speak past a whisper, and her voice was hoarse.

After Lucross had been shot on Ka Hale, he and the team were gathered and transported to Pan aboard Alterous' *Leviathan*. Lucross was admitted into the Margin Military Hospital, and operations began almost immediately.

The bullet had passed straight through his body, barely missing his heart and puncturing his left lung. It was a surprise to most everyone that he had survived and, after hours of operation, was recovering.

Chris, Amabel and James stood next to Lucross' unconscious body, watching as a machine filled his lungs with air. Amabel was trying her damnedest to hold herself together.

"What have they found from the investigation?" Chris asked James.

"They haven't had too long t'look," James sighed, wiping sweat from his forehead. "But so far, almost nothin'.

The shot was taken from the north with an S-44. Other than that, the shooter was clean."

Amabel shook, finding it harder to keep her walls from tumbling down. Chris felt terrible for her, watching as the tears dripped from her chin.

He knew exactly what it felt like to lose a lover.

"We need to let him rest," Chris said, putting his hand on her shoulder.

She flinched at his touch, but he didn't pull away.

"Come on, Amabel," James said. "Let's go."

They turned away, and Chris took one last mournful look at Lucross before they exited the room. Katherine and Samantha were in the hallway beyond, Samantha comforting Katherine as Chris and the others went to meet with them.

"Let's go back to the barracks," Chris said as he began to lead the way out of the hospital. They moved through silently, the only sounds were the tears from Amabel and Katherine dripping to the floor.

A car waited outside for them, ready to take the team wherever they needed to be. They filed in, and Chris told the driver to take them home.

The barracks on Pan were not as large or luxurious as those of the Easter Island base back on Earth, but they were suited enough. Chris and the others did not plan to stay for long, despite Lucross' condition.

Back inside apartment-like barracks, each member of Alpha team went about their own activities. They remained within eyesight of one another, knowing that any of them could break down without warning.

Chris lamented for Lucross. He had never had such a feeling of vulnerability as any normal human being. The closest he had felt was on the Terran flagship, but even then, he healed.

Unfortunately, there would be no miracles to bring Lucross back to his full potential so quickly. Lucross would be lucky enough to function the same after such an attack. Chris debated a prayer, but he knew full well that God didn't intend to listen to him. There was nothing Chris could do for Lucross, unless he were to reveal himself in full.

No, he thought. *I can't do that. Not yet. Lucross will just have to heal on his own.*

When Chris made the agreement to come to the physical realm, he left a large segment of his true form behind. However, part of the pact called for a reinstatement of that destructive power if Chris ever deemed it necessary to complete his mission.

Chris was ashamed to think it, but he knew that whether Lucross lived or died did not matter in the grand operation.

"I think we should retire," Amabel said, her voice cutting through the thoughts Chris wished to evade. She was sitting on the couch with her head between her knees, as though she were trying to remain as small as possible.

"What?" James said. He swung around from the computer screen he had dug himself into.

"Why would you say that?" Samantha asked. Katherine remained silent, sitting next to Chris shyly.

"We've done our duty," Amabel said plainly, her face lacking any real emotion. Confusion flooded over the faces of her friends. "Don't you guys see how dangerous our job is? We've fought more than anyone else in that damn war. Lucross and I dedicated our lives to keeping the universe safe. But one of these days, this 'commitment' we've pledged will be the end of us."

"Amabel," Chris interjected, "calm down. We're all going to be fine."

"Yes," Katherine agreed tentatively. "The war is over. There won't be any more danger."

"Are you really such a fool to think that?" Amabel yelled, her walls breaking. "War never ends! We defeated the army, not the ideal. Any empire that ends is left splintered, not defeated. Where one is overthrown, at least five more could take its place!"

"Do not yell at Katherine," Chris said, irritation building inside of him. "You don't know what's going to happen. None of us do."

"Hundreds of billions of people died during that fucking war," she continued, ignoring Chris' warning. "You really think we're so special? That we're immortal? We're nothing more than ants, you dolt! All of us are fragile, and the fighting will never stop." Katherine began to sob. "Do you not remember what happened after the Solar War? The chaos that ensued afterwards? We're going to die!"

"*Amabel!*" Chris yelled, rising to his feet and slamming his fist on the table next to him. Katherine ran back to her room, crying along the way. Chris watched as she disappeared from his view, then turned back to Amabel. His eyes were flaring a dark purple, and it was apparent that she noticed.

"I'm sorry…" she shied back, curling up into a ball.

"Just because Lucross was shot, doesn't mean it's the end of the world, or the end of us." Chris' voice was smooth, so calm that it appeared to shake Amabel to her core. "If you choose to abandon your friends, good on you. But don't you *dare* take your grief out on us."

"You're right…I'm sorry." Chris' eyes cooled, his anger receding.

"I think we both know that Katherine deserves an apology."

James and Samantha watched on in awed silence as Amabel stood and made her way to Katherine's room. Nobody had ever seen Chris so angry before. He was quick to admit to himself that he had never been so furious.

"Chris," James said. "Are you okay?"

"I'm fine." That was all he said before walking back to his room and shutting the door.

Just as he had done so, his communicator began to beep erratically. Picking it up, he answered it and lifted it to his head.

"Hello?" he said.

"*Christopher? It is Sargent,*" Alterous' voice cracked through.

"What can I do for you?"

"*I need you and your team to come to the command center. You are being reassigned.*" His voice was calm, so Chris could tell they weren't in any danger.

"We'll head over as soon as we can." Chris wasn't in the mood to talk, and he was sure Alterous could detect it.

"*Alright. Alterous out.*"

The line disconnected, and Chris strapped his communicator to his wrist. He walked out of his room once more, where everyone had already gathered once again. They seemed surprised to see him out of his room so quickly.

"I just got off the line with Alterous," he said as he approached them. "We're being reassigned, and he wants us to report to the command center immediately."

"Did he tell you what he wants us to do?" Samantha asked.

"No. Now let's go."

They all grabbed their belongings and left the barracks for the control center.

#

"It is good to see that you're all doing well," Alterous said as they entered the main room. "I am sure it has been a tough time, but I know you all can push through." Amabel shied back a bit, knowing well that she was struggling to keep in shape.

"What's the new assignment, sir?" Chris said, changing the subject to alleviate the awkwardness.

"You are a very talented group of people, Alpha. All experts in your fields. You will be glad to know that this next assignment will not be a field mission. You will be staying right here, on Pan." The news was a bit shocking, and Alterous paused to let it sink in. "Instead," he continued, "your next assignment will be to help me."

"Sir?" James said, unsure.

"You all fought to bring peace to our division, and thereby to the worlds it held. Now, we need to maintain that peace and reassume control and diplomacy on our colonies. We need to begin rebuilding, and I want you all to help me."

"How can we do that?" Katherine asked.

"Like I said, you're all experts. Strategy, military placements, and so on. Your presence alone helps to inspire people. Our division could use some of that inspiration, don't you think?" The group remained silent, but nodded in response. Chris knew they wouldn't admit it, but they were glad they didn't have to leave Pan.

Chris, however, was glad that he'd be working with his old friend once again.

"Also," Alterous said. "Christopher."

"Sir?"

"I'm promoting you as Commander of Alpha until Stone recovers." Chris' heart skipped a beat when the command was given. It had been so long since he had been the leader of anyone, and he was severely out of practice.

"Yes sir!" he exclaimed, failing at an attempt to keep his excitement to himself. He smiled as his eyes brightened.

"You will start tomorrow. Report back at sunrise. Dismissed."

The team saluted and filed out, but Chris stayed behind and stood with Alterous.

"It's a good thing you assigned this to my team," Chris said. "They need time to recover emotionally, and putting them in the field would only cause more pain and disarray."

"Hey, it is the least I can do for an old friend."

"Thank you." Chris looked at the data table in front of them, scanning through the open files and reports from different planets. "Looks like we'll be working together again. You sure you're okay with keeping my higher intellect around?"

"I am sure I will manage," Alterous chuckled. "Your political and militaristic divinity will definitely be used."

"I'll see what I can do. I'm a bit out of practice."

"You will be fine, Christopher. And this way, we will be able to squeeze a drink or two in together. Catch up a little, now that peace has settled."

"I'll make sure it happens." Chris held out his hand to Alterous, who took it gratefully and shook it with respect. Releasing his grip, Chris made his way out of the command center. "It's good to be back, Sargent!" he called back, his smile broad.

He decided to walk back to the barracks, ignoring the offers for a ride. His mood was too great, and almost nothing could take it down.

On this day, Chris realized something. He saw, for the first time, just who his true mission really effects. All the shattered worlds and lives, all the people he had worked to save. And now, he would work to save them again.

To save all of humanity.

It was as a wise man once said about his species: "For all our failings, despite our limitations and fallibilities, we humans are capable of greatness."

And for a final time, Chris was convinced of his performance. He would bring the human race to its golden age, before returning home to God.

22

19th January 2754 15:47:39

The space station *Autumn* revolved around the beta rift with a blinding brilliance. Its silvery white exterior reflected the rays the rift expelled, causing it to shine like a cosmic diamond.

The station was modeled after that which had been built for the study of alpha rift before it had grown to an unexpected size. The *Autumn* had been constructed during the period between the Solar Assault and the Cessation, for the sole purpose of analyzing and gathering information about the status and properties of beta rift.

Falkner sat at his desk in the small room he called an office, staring at a picture of his dad. His father had helped to design the device used to create the rift, though Falkner had not been informed of this until recently.

He had been contacted on the tenth of November; the day that beta rift had been opened. The crack could be seen all the way from Earth, and Falkner had already begun making observations. After a long discussion with the First Councilor of the Council of Earth, Falkner agreed to work as the lead scientist on the *Autumn*.

"*Professor Augustine?*" the voice of his assistant buzzed through his communicator.

"Yes, Mellissa?" he said, pulling his eyes away from his dad's picture.

"*The data from this morning has been sorted and sent to you.*"

"Thank you, darling." He turned off his communicator and swung to face his computer. Part of his job was to look over the data gathered from researchers across the station.

The screen booted, and he pulled up the new files, as well as some older ones. He had a rhythm of comparing newer data to older sets to make sure nothing had changed between the two dates. In this instance, he had decided to use the set of variables from the day after the station had been commissioned.

Scanning his eyes over the document, he noticed that two sets of elements that had a distinctly significant difference. According to the new figures, the Energy Output and Time Distortion traits of beta had expanded by one hundred-fold.

What was once measured in the hundreds now reached to the thousands.

A knock at Falkner's door startled him, the metal slab sliding to reveal a man.

"Professor Augustine," the man, Dr. Michael Kneed, said. "You need to come see this. It's urgent!" Dr. Kneed seemed very alarmed, and Falkner jumped from his seat to see the matter.

"What is it, Mike?" Falkner asked as he walked passed Dr. Kneed and out of the office.

"You need to see it for yourself. The rift. Observation deck."

The two proceeded through the maze of corridors inside of the Autumn. Michael didn't bother to slow down, the urgent business seemingly driving him forward. One final left turn, and they reached the doors to the observation deck.

Dr. Kneed wasted no time swiping his key card, unlocking the doors and striding in, with Falkner close behind. On the deck, a dozen or more of the other scientists and staff members had already gathered in the open air, and were staring blankly in the direction of beta. Only two of them noticed Falkner walk out among them.

Follow their gaze, Falkner slowly found himself staring into beta rift. When his eyes locked on it, he lost all feeling in his body.

The rift was shining brighter than before, with more intensity than the light from the galactic center. Bolts of lightning shot off in every direction, their range just short of the *Autumn*'s hull. An incredible feat and display of power, considering the five-hundred kilometer distance between the station and the mass of time energy.

The space around the rift and bolts of energy seemed to distort as well. Distant stars seemed to twist and fade before popping back into existence.

"How long has this been going on for?" Falkner asked Michael, whose eyes were glued to the anomaly in front of them.

"We assume all morning, sir," Michael responded. "Nobody noticed until one of the bolts knocked the power from the east wing of the station."

Falkner continued to stare into the beta rift, its power and light bathing him.

"Everyone, get back inside," he said hurriedly. "Conduct more thorough tests." As the people began to move, a strike of electricity knocked into the east wing of the *Autumn*. One of the many rooms exploded as the lights aboard the station flickered. The crew began to panic, unsure of what to do in such an event.

"Everyone, continue on with your duties!" Falkner pulled his communicator out of his jacket and quickly turned it on. "Mellissa," he said into the device, "tell the captain to increase the distance between the *Autumn* and beta rift, and get me a line with the Council of Earth immediately."

"*Yes sir,*" Mellissa said before the line was cut.

His communicator beeped as the station began to recede further into space. He answered and began walking back across the observation deck.

"Councilor Jackson, this is Professor Falkner Augustine of the Beta Rift Research Station. We've got a problem." Falkner looked back at the rift before he continued through the doorway. "Sir, beta rift has become unstable."

ABOUT THE AUTHOR

Christian Brinkman began writing as a high school freshman, inspired by his friends to create a world he could call his own. Pursuing a writing career and motivated to become a software engineer, his goals in life make him the protagonist of his own story. He can often be found reading, writing, or calmly enjoying life. Christian currently lives in Hawaii.

Made in the USA
Middletown, DE
23 August 2022

71286777R10169